Ready To Blow

"Mr. Adams," Chief Coleman said, "do you know what your friend Mr. Fitzgerald does here in Tucson?"

"No," Clint said. "That's one of the things I was going to find out. I know, in the past, he's been in charge of running some business. His talent seems to be in management."

"Exactly," Coleman said. "Mr. Fitzgerald is in charge of building the new university outside of town."

"The University of Arizona," Sheriff Leland said. "He probably got held up by one of the problems that have been popping up."

"Wait," Clint said. "University? Problems?"

"You see, Tucson was awarded twenty-five thousand dollars to build the University of Arizona."

"While Phoenix," Leland said, "was awarded a hundred thousand dollars to build a new insane asylum."

Clint stared at both of them and said, "That hardly seems fair."

"That is what some people in town seem to think," Coleman said.

"So there have been problems out there," Leland said. "Fires, damage . . . everybody's waiting for the big boom."

"Boom?" Clint asked.

"So much has been happening, the only thing left is to . . . blow it up."

THE GUNSMITH

368

THE UNIVERSITY SHOWDOWN

J. R. ROBERTS

JOVE BOOKS, NEW YORK

THE BERKLEY PUBLISHING GROUP
Published by the Penguin Group
Penguin Group (USA) Inc.
375 Hudson Street, New York, New York 10014, USA

Penguin Group (Canada), 90 Eglinton Avenue East, Suite 700, Toronto, Ontario M4P 2Y3, Canada
(a division of Pearson Penguin Canada Inc.) • Penguin Books Ltd., 80 Strand, London WC2R 0RL,
England • Penguin Group Ireland, 25 St. Stephen's Green, Dublin 2, Ireland (a division of Penguin
Books Ltd.) • Penguin Group (Australia), 250 Camberwell Road, Camberwell, Victoria 3124, Australia
(a division of Pearson Australia Group Pty. Ltd.) • Penguin Books India Pvt. Ltd., 11 Community
Centre, Panchsheel Park, New Delhi—110 017, India • Penguin Group (NZ), 67 Apollo Drive,
Rosedale, Auckland 0632, New Zealand (a division of Pearson New Zealand Ltd.) • Penguin Books
(South Africa) (Pty.) Ltd., 24 Sturdee Avenue, Rosebank, Johannesburg 2196, South Africa

Penguin Books Ltd., Registered Offices: 80 Strand, London WC2R 0RL, England

This is a work of fiction. Names, characters, places, and incidents either are the product of the author's
imagination or are used fictitiously, and any resemblance to actual persons, living or dead, business
establishments, events, or locales is entirely coincidental.

THE UNIVERSITY SHOWDOWN

A Jove Book / published by arrangement with the author

PUBLISHING HISTORY
Jove edition / August 2012

ISBN: 978-0-515-15105-3

JOVE®
Jove Books are published by The Berkley Publishing Group,
a division of Penguin Group (USA) Inc.,
375 Hudson Street, New York, New York 10014.
JOVE® is a registered trademark of Penguin Group (USA) Inc.
The "J" design is a trademark of Penguin Group (USA) Inc.

PRINTED IN THE UNITED STATES OF AMERICA

10 9 8 7 6 5 4 3 2 1

ALWAYS LEARNING **PEARSON**

ONE

When Clint Adams rode into Tucson, Arizona, he was thinking about the Earp Brothers. It was at the Tucson railway station that Wyatt killed Frank Stilwell, who was responsible for the shooting death of Morgan Earp in Tombstone. Wyatt then sent his family to the safety of California while he continued to hunt down the remainder of the Clanton faction from the O.K. Corral. Clint was in Tombstone with the Earps and Doc Holliday during the O.K. Corral, but he had not accompanied his friend to Tucson, and didn't go with Wyatt on his ride for vengeance.

As had become his wont in life of late, Clint was riding into Tucson at the behest of a friend. A man like Clint Adams made a lot of friends over the years, and when they put out a call for help, he responded. There had been a few occasions over the years when he'd needed help, put out a call, and his friends had responded. It was simply not in him to turn a deaf ear to a call for help. Or if not help, then at least advice.

The fact was, he never knew what to expect when he responded in these instances. Telegrams were really not able to carry all the facts of a call for help, beyond the word HELP.

He rode into Tucson, which had grown by leaps and bounds since his last visit. Riding down the main street, he passed the building that housed the Tucson Police Department. Tucson was one of the first Western towns to turn their law enforcement responsibilities over to a police department rather than a sheriff or marshal. It had been in existence for almost eight years.

He continued on, past the now deserted marshal's office, and the sheriff's office. The sheriff was now more of a politician than a lawman. Clint hoped he'd have no contact with either the police or the sheriff, but that hope was not realistic. Not for a man with his reputation.

He finally reached the livery stable, went through the motions of having Eclipse cared for, carrying his saddlebags and rifle to a nearby hotel and getting himself a room.

Once he had a room, he dumped his things on the bed and looked out the window at the busy Tucson street.

He shook his head. How much trouble was he walking into this time?

David Darling, mayor of Tucson, looked up and down the table at the members of his town council.

"This is not a matter that should be open for discussion at this point, gentlemen," he said. "The decision was made years ago by the Territorial Legislative Assembly."

"The Thieving Thirteen," Andrew Leland said.

"Enough of that," Darling said.

"Come on, Mayor," Ed Romine said. "You know there were backroom deals made during that Assembly. A thief is a thief in my book."

"Look," Darling said, "Phoenix got the hundred thousand dollars for the insane asylum, and we got the twenty-five thousand for the university."

"A school," Sheriff Leland said. "Call it was it is. We got a goddamned school."

"Universities are respected institutions back East," Chief of Police Robert Coleman said. "Shouldn't be any different here."

"And who's gonna want to go to school here when they can go back East?" Leland asked.

"Plenty of people," Darling said. "Look, let's get back to the subject at hand. Can the police department handle the threats and incidents that have been happening, or do we need to hire someone privately?"

"The police can handle anything," Chief Coleman said. "I assure you."

"Do you?" George Eiland asked. Eiland was the representative from the university, who had come to the council to ask for help. "We've already had fires, vandalism, water damage—what are we waiting for, someone to blow the building up even before it's finished?"

"Chief?" the mayor asked, looking at Coleman.

"We're investigating, Mayor," Coleman said. "I have my best men on the case."

"When can we expect to see some results?" Darling asked.

"Very soon."

The mayor looked at Eiland and asked, "George?"

"That's not good enough for us, Mayor," Eiland said. "Not by a long sight."

"I'm afraid it will have to be," the mayor said. "For now."

Eiland looked crestfallen.

The mayor banged his gavel and said, "This meeting is adjourned."

The council members stood, gathered their papers, and began to leave, some of them arranging to meet for drinks somewhere.

George Eiland slunk unhappily from the room, alone. He was going to have to go back to his dean and explain the situation.

The room emptied quickly, leaving only the mayor and the chief.

"Bob," Darling said, "I'm gonna need those results, you know. And soon."

"My best detective is on it, Mayor."

"One man?"

"He's very experienced and committed," Coleman said. "And he can have all the help he needs, whenever he needs it."

"I'm not going to be able to wait much longer," Darling said.

"You can depend on me, Mayor," Coleman said.

"I hope so."

The chief left the room, passing another man on the way.

"Mayor," Dennis Fairman said.

"What, Dennis?" the mayor said. "Don't give me any bad news."

"I don't know if it's good or bad."

The mayor sighed heavily.

"Okay, tell me."

"Clint Adams rode into town today," Fairman said. "He got himself a room at the Congress Hotel."

The mayor sat down heavily—which, considering his weight, was the way he always sat down.

"The Gunsmith is in Tucson?" he asked. "What else can happen?"

Fairman didn't know what to say to that, so he simply waited.

"Was he met by anyone?"

"No."

"So we don't know if he's here by coincidence, or if someone sent for him."

"No, we don't."

"Well, then find out, Dennis," the mayor said. "That's the kind of thing I pay you to know, isn't it?"

"Well . . . yes, sir."

"Then get out of here," the mayor said, "and do your job."

"Yessir."

Jesus, the mayor thought, the goddamned Gunsmith. The town still hadn't recovered from Wyatt Earp's killing of Frank Stilwell, and now the Gunsmith was in town. What next?

TWO

Clint came down from his room, left the hotel, and went looking for a place to eat. He didn't ask the desk clerk for help. Invariably, hotel desk clerks steered people to whatever restaurant was kicking back money to them. Clint decided to trust his own nose to find a place to eat.

He found a small café a few blocks from the hotel, across the street from the abandoned marshal's office. He stopped in front, took a deep breath, and decided this was the place. Among all the cooking meat smells was the overpowering aroma of strong coffee.

He got seated at a back table. As busy as the streets were at 3 p.m., the café was only half full. Most people were working, not eating.

"What can I getcha, sir?" the waiter asked.

"I smell some strong coffee," Clint said. "I'll start with a pot of that."

"Yessir. Comin' up."

The other folks in the place glanced over at the stranger, talked among themselves, wondering who he was, but eventually went back to their meals.

The waiter brought the coffee, which was as hot and strong as it smelled. As Clint took a sip, the waiter started walking away.

"Hey, don't go anywhere," Clint said.

"Sir?"

"Steak, bloody, with everything."

"Yes, sir."

Clint looked at the clock on the wall. He had a six o'clock appointment in the hotel lobby. He had plenty of time to enjoy his meal and then check out the town, which was something he always did. Might even stop in at the police department and present himself. Sometimes that avoided trouble.

While most of the diners had gone back to their meals, there was one who still seemed interested in him. A woman, seated with a man whose back was to him. She was blond, with striking blue eyes and a firm jaw. More handsome than pretty. But very attractive.

The waiter brought his steak and Clint asked, "Who's the blond woman with the blue eyes?"

The waiter looked, but he knew who Clint meant.

"That is Mrs. Cynthia Bodeen. And the man with her is her husband, Patrick." The waiter leaned in. "He's the jealous type."

"Does he have reason to be?"

"Usually."

"Thanks."

"Enjoy your meal."

Clint did.

* * *

Halfway through his meal the Bodeens finished and stood up. The man dropped some money on the table, and then they seemed to get into an argument.

"Not this again," the man said loudly.

"Well, what do you expect, darling?"

"I expect you to act like a wife, sometime."

She laughed and said, "And I expect you to act like a man. We're both doomed to disappointment."

"Bitch!" he said, and stormed out.

Other diners averted their eyes, as if they were used to this kind of behavior from these two people. The blond woman shook her head and walked over to Clint's table. He could see that she was tall and well formed and, up close, just a bit older than he'd thought, maybe forty.

She stood there and stared at Clint. He looked up at her.

"Very smart of you," he said.

"What was?"

"To wait until your husband paid the bill before fighting with him."

"He pays all my bills, whether we're fighting or not," she said, "and we're always fighting. You haven't asked, but may I sit down?"

"Excuse me for being rude," he said. "Yes, please sit down."

She sat across from him.

"Are you the welcoming committee?" he asked.

"Not for every stranger who comes to town," she said, "just the interesting-looking ones."

"I'm flattered."

"Please," she said, "keep eating. I didn't mean to interrupt your meal. I just wanted to introduce myself."

"The waiter told me who you were," Clint said. "Cynthia Bodeen."

"Then you have the advantage over me," she said. "Who are you?"

"My name is Clint Adams."

She sat back in her chair, but looked delighted rather than shocked.

"I know that name."

"Do you?"

"The Gunsmith, right?"

"That's me."

She started to laugh.

"What's so funny?" he asked.

"This is rich," she said, shaking her head. "You are going to shake up everybody in town."

"Why's that?"

"You don't know what's been going on in this county, do you?" she asked. "Or do you?"

"I have no idea."

"Then why are you here?"

"Just passing through."

"That's too much of a coincidence," she said.

"You think so?" He put a chunk of steak in his mouth. "Would you like me to get you something? A piece of pie maybe?"

"Oh, no," she said. "I've got to watch my figure."

"Oh, I bet all the men in town do that for you," he commented.

"Why, thank you, Mr. Adams," she said. "I can see I'm going to have to watch out for you. A man who knows how to speak to a woman is dangerous."

"You know," he said, "you were going to tell me what's going on in town? And the county?"

"Was I?"

"I thought you were."

She folded her arms and regarded him across the table.

"I don't know," she said. "Maybe not."

"Why not?"

"Because I don't think you're passing through," she said, "and I don't think you're as clueless as you make out."

She stood up.

"Where are you going?" he asked.

"I have things to do," she said, "but we'll see each other again. Count on it."

"Cynthia—"

"You're meeting someone in town," she said. "Somebody who sent for you. They're going to tell you all you need to know."

"Will they tell me about you and your husband?" he asked.

She laughed, leaned over, and said in a low voice, "All you need to know, Mr. Adams."

THREE

After he'd finished his meal, Clint left the café and took a walk around town. Cynthia Bodeen—whoever she was—had piqued his interest. Apparently she thought something was going on in town that his presence would affect. His 6 p.m. meeting would probably supply all the answers he needed, but he decided to have a couple of drinks, visit different saloons, keep his ears open, and see what he could find out for himself.

He stopped in a small saloon called The Haven Saloon, nursed a beer, but didn't get much in the way of conversation. Most of the patrons there seemed interested in drinking and little else.

When he got to a larger saloon, called Hanigan's Saloon, the men were more talkative, but all he got was bragging, threats, and comments about some of the town's women.

He finished his beer, though, and was about to leave when he heard the name "Bodeen." Two men standing at the end of the bar were talking.

"Now there's a woman I'd like to get to know," one man said.

"Not much chance of that, Tim," another man said. "She's way out of your league."

"You think so," the man called Tim asked. "Believe me, from what I hear, she ain't that much of a lady."

"She's married to one of the richest men in the county," his friend said.

Tim laughed. "And that makes her a lady? Them two is so different it's amazin' they're still married."

"He ain't about to let a woman like that go," the other man said. "Not a woman like her."

Tim stared at his friend.

"Are you tryin' ta make me think that you been with her?"

"Not me," the other man said, "but I know a man who was. He says she's a animal. Tore his back to ribbons with her nails."

"Yeah? That's the kinda woman I like."

"Yeah, right," the other man said. "You get a scratch and you're runnin' to the doc."

From that point on, they just seemed to be insulting each other's manhood, so Clint left and headed back to his hotel.

He went back up to his room to wash his face and hands, but then went back down to the lobby to wait for his friend to arrive. By six thirty, he started to worry, and by seven, he figured he was going to have to start asking questions—even though he'd been asked not to.

He took the telegrams out and read them again. The first asked for help. When he answered that one, the second set up the meeting at the hotel on this day—and it asked him not to talk to anyone ahead of time.

He refolded them and put them away. Now what should he do? He needed to look for his friend, but who should he ask? Bartenders and desk clerks, or the police? Given his friend's position in town, maybe the police were the best bet.

He hadn't taken the time to stop into the police station before, so maybe that was the way to go now. Drop in, introduce himself, and when they inevitably asked him what he was doing there, drop his friend's name and see what the reaction was.

He left the hotel and headed for the police station.

FOUR

"And your name is what again?" the sergeant behind the desk asked.

"Clint Adams."

"And you want to see the chief?"

"Yes."

"Do you know him?"

"I've never met him."

"Then why do you want to see him?"

"Just to let him know that I'm in town."

The young sergeant frowned at Clint and asked him, "Why would he want to know you're in town, sir?"

Clint studied the man. After all these years of maybe wanting to meet someone who had no idea who he was, had he just done it? At the wrong time?

"Look, Sergeant," he said, "if you'll just tell your chief I'm here, I'm sure he'll want—"

"I can't bother the chief right now, sir," the sergeant

said. "If you'll tell me what your problem is, I can have the right person talk to you."

"You're not from here, are you?" Clint asked.

"And by here, you mean . . ."

"The West?"

"No, sir," the man young man said. "I've only just come out from back East to take this job."

"I see."

The sergeant waited, and then said, "So? The problem? You want to report something?"

"Actually," Clint said, "no. I'd just like you to write down my name and the fact that I was here. Then I'll be on my way."

"Well . . . all right." The man looked as if he was writing. Actually, he could have just been doodling to appease Clint. "Adams, right?"

"That's right."

"Okay, sir," he said, "I have it down."

Clint considered telling the sergeant that he wanted to report a missing person, but he didn't know for sure his friend was missing. He was simply a little more than an hour overdue for a meeting.

"Thank you, Sergeant."

"Yes, sir," the man said. "I'm pleased to have helped."

Clint turned and left the police station.

He walked around town, wondering if he should simply have demanded to see the chief. Or at least, someone in authority. But the fact of the matter was, he had been at the police station trying to report his own arrival in town, and the policeman at the front desk had not had the slightest interest. Was that his fault? No.

As he was walking, he realized he was across the street from the sheriff's office. Since there was still a sheriff, he figured why not stop in there. At the very least the man might know where his friend was.

He crossed the street, and entered.

"Sheriff?" he asked the man at the desk.

The desk was pushed up against the wall, and the seated man had to turn around to see him. He looked like a storekeeper, or an accountant, but was wearing a sheriff's badge pinned to his vest. Beneath the vest he was wearing a white shirt, and a bow tie. His hair was sparse and fair, and he had a bushy mustache that hid his mouth—and his age. Clint thought he could be thirty, or fifty.

"Yes?"

"You are the sheriff?" Clint asked.

"That's right. Sheriff Leland. What can I do for you, friend?"

"Sheriff, my name is Clint Adams, and I've come to town to see a friend of mine, Ted Fitzgerald."

"Fitzgerald."

"That's right. Do you know him?"

"I know you, sir."

"Well, that's good, I suppose," Clint said. "I went over to the police station and they didn't seem to have any idea who I am."

"Is that a fact?" That seemed to amuse the sheriff. He stood up, revealing himself to be no more than five feet six or so. "Can I offer you a cup of coffee?"

"No, thank you. I've had my breakfast."

"Who did you talk to at the police department?"

"A young sergeant, I didn't get his name. He was at the front desk."

"Ah, so you didn't get to see the chief?"

"No, the sergeant didn't see any reason to let me see him."

"Do you still want to?" Leland asked. "I could introduce you."

Clint could see that the sheriff was very anxious for him to say yes. He thought if he allowed the sheriff to take him over to the police station, it might give him some idea of the dynamic that existed between the police and Sheriff Leland.

"Sure," Clint said, "why not? It might be interesting to go back there."

"I think it'll be very interesting."

FIVE

On the way back to the police station, Clint told Leland that he was supposed to meet Ted Fitzgerald in the hotel lobby at six.

"Do you have some business with him?" Leland asked.

"We're friends," Clint said. "I sent a telegram that I was passing through, and he agreed to meet me in the hotel."

"He did not appear?"

"He did not."

"Is that why you were going to the police?"

"It was one reason," Clint said. "I don't think I can report him missing, but I thought they might be able to tell me where to find him."

"I can tell you that," Leland said, "but let's wait until after we see the chief."

When they reached the police station, they entered and stopped just inside the door.

"Is that the sergeant you were talking to?" Leland asked.

"Yes, that's him."

"Come on."

They approached the desk and the young sergeant looked at them, then at the badge on the sheriff's vest. He didn't seem to notice that Clint was back again.

"Sergeant, I'd like to see Chief Coleman, please."

"Do you have an appointment, Sheriff?" the sergeant asked.

"No, but if you tell him I'm here, I'm sure he'll see me."

"Sir, I can't just interrupt the chief—"

"That's what he told me, too," Clint said, cutting the man off.

Now the sergeant looked at Clint and realized that he had seen him before.

"Oh, you're back."

"Yes, I am."

"I see," the sergeant said. "Did you think that by returning here with the sheriff, I would be forced to let you see the chief?"

"Not at all," Clint said. "In fact, it wasn't even my idea to come back here."

"I insisted on bringing Mr. Adams over here to introduce him to the chief," Sheriff Leland said.

"Mr. Adams?" Clint was now sure the man had never written down his name.

"Yes, Clint Adams," Leland said. "Sergeant, are you going to try to tell me you don't know who this man is?"

The sergeant blinked, looked at Clint and Leland in turn. It was starting to dawn on him that maybe he had made an error in judgment somewhere along the way.

"I'm sorry, but no . . ."

"Well, if you had told your chief he was here," Leland said, "he would have told you who he was."

"My job is to—"

"So if you'll tell the chief now that I'm here, with Clint Adams, I'm sure he'll see us."

"Well . . . just wait here a minute."

The sergeant went into the bowels of the building while Clint and the sheriff waited.

"There are more and more of these buildings going up in the West," Clint said, "and they all seem to be the same."

"I agree."

"I'll bet I could even find my way to the chief's office."

Suddenly, from somewhere inside the building, they heard a man shouting.

"I don't think you'll have to do that, Mr. Adams," Leland said.

Moments later the sergeant reappeared, his face red, as if he were having a heart attack.

"Gentlemen," he said, "if you'll follow me? The chief will see you now."

SIX

The young sergeant led them through the building to the chief's office. As they passed other police officers, they all turned their heads away and would not look at the sergeant.

When they reached the office, the sergeant said, "Chief, Sheriff Leland and Mr. . . . Mr. Adams."

"Chief," Leland said as he entered.

"Sheriff," Chief Coleman said, "I'm sorry you were kept waiting."

"It's not me, so much as Mr. Adams, here," Leland said. "Clint Adams, meet Chief Robert Coleman."

"Mr. Adams," Coleman said, "a pleasure."

Leland and Coleman looked like they had been plucked out of the same litter. It wasn't so much that they resembled each other—the chief was taller, huskier—but they seemed to be two sides of the same coin. Clint wondered if they were hired at the same time. Leland didn't seem to have the demeanor of a longtime sheriff who was being replaced by a modern police department.

"Chief." The two men shook hands.

"My sergeant's an idiot," the chief said. "The town council made me hire some men from the East, and they don't know their asses from a donkey. Please, both of you. Have a seat."

They sat down.

"What brings you to Tucson, Mr. Adams?"

"I'm looking for a friend of mine."

"Oh? Who's that?"

"Ted Fitzgerald."

He saw the chief look at the sheriff.

"Mr. Adams was supposed to meet Mr. Fitzgerald in his hotel lobby at six p.m., but Mr. Fitzgerald never appeared."

"Is that right?"

"What do you two gentlemen know that I don't?" Clint asked. "Where is Ted?"

"Mr. Adams," Chief Coleman said, "do you know what your friend Mr. Fitzgerald does here in Tucson?"

"No," Clint said. "That's one of the things I was going to find out. I know, in the past, he's been in charge of running some business. His talent seems to be in management."

"Exactly," Coleman said. "Mr. Fitzgerald is in charge of building the new university outside of town."

"The University of Arizona," Sheriff Leland said. "He probably got held up by one of the problems that have been popping up."

"Wait," Clint said. "University? Problems?"

"You see, Tucson was awarded twenty-five thousand dollars to build the University of Arizona."

"While Phoenix," Leland said, "was awarded a hundred thousand dollars to build a new insane asylum."

Clint stared at both of them and said, "That hardly seems fair."

"That is what some people in town seem to think," Coleman said.

"So there have been problems out there," Leland said. "Fires, damage . . . everybody's waiting for the big boom."

"Boom?" Clint asked.

"So much has been happening the only thing left is to . . . blow it up."

Clint looked at Chief Coleman.

"Is this for real?"

"Well . . . not really," Coleman said, "and then . . . maybe."

"And what are you doing about it?" Clint asked.

"I've got my best man working on it," Coleman said. "He's a top detective. We were lucky to get him to come here."

"From where?" Clint asked.

"Back East. Philadelphia."

"You've got a Philadelphia detective working on this?" Clint asked.

"The difference between the East and the West is not as big as it once was, Mr. Adams," Coleman said. There are many towns and cities out here with modern police departments, using modern techniques."

"And how have your modern techniques done so far?" Clint asked.

Coleman sat back in his chair and said, "We're still working on it."

Clint looked at Leland.

"Don't look at me," he said. "I'm not an Old West sheriff. I'm a politician here. I've got little to say about how the law gets enforced. That's all up to Chief Coleman here."

"Okay, well, I'm only concerned with finding Ted Fitzgerald."

"I can take you to him," Leland said. "If he didn't come in to meet you, then he's out there."

"Out there?"

"At the site," Leland said, "where they're building the university."

"How far?"

"Couple of hours."

"It'll be dark by then," Clint said.

"I know the way," Leland said, "and it's all main road."

Clint looked at the wall clock. It was seven thirty.

"I want to check my hotel again first," he said. "Maybe he's late. Maybe I overreacted."

"Sure, check the hotel again," Leland said. "Wait till tomorrow, even. I can take you out there, or give you directions."

Clint looked at Coleman.

"These incidents of fires, damage," he asked, "had anyone been hurt?"

"No," Coleman said, then added, "not yet."

Clint got to his feet.

"Thank you for seeing me," he said, "both of you. I think I'll take my chances here in town tonight. If I have to, I'll ride out there tomorrow. Main road, you say?"

"Due east," Leland said. "You can't miss it."

Clint nodded and left.

SEVEN

When Clint got back to his hotel, he found Ted Fitzgerald waiting in the lobby.

"The desk clerk told me you were here," Fitzgerald said as they shook hands.

"Well, you've always been so punctual, I panicked when you didn't show up at six."

Fitzgerald laughed.

"I've never seen you panic about anything. Where've you been?"

"The sheriff's office, the police station."

"Did you meet the chief?"

"I did."

"Then they told you what's been going on."

"Some."

"Okay, well," Fitzgerald, said, "I'll fill you in the rest of the way. Let's get a drink."

They went into the hotel's saloon, which was small

and basically just used by guests. There were too many other saloons in town for it to attract much local business. But it would do for them.

Armed with a beer each, they went to a table and sat. Fitzgerald was in his fifties, and if he actually was in charge of building the university, it was the biggest job he'd ever had.

"I'm directing the action," he told Clint. "We had an architect—"

"Let's go back further," Clint said.

"The legislature was supposed to meet to decide who got what. The jewel was the hundred thousand dollars allocated for building a mental institution. We're in Pima County. The Pima County contingent ran into a flooding Salt River. By the time they found another route to Prescott, the deals had been made. That money changed hands under the table, or in a back room, there is no doubt. Pima County did not get the hundred thousand for the mental hospital. They got twenty-five thousand to build Arizona's first university."

"And they would have preferred to have an insane asylum outside of town?"

"They would have preferred to have the hundred thousand," Fitzgerald said. "More money to skim off the top."

"So people are upset."

"To say the least. But they hired an architect, and they hired me to oversee the project. I got held up on the site, or I would have been here at six."

"They told me about some . . . what? Sabotage?"

"That's as good as any definition of what's been going on," Fitzgerald said. "I need help, Clint. I need somebody to watch my back."

"The chief told me he's got his best man on the job," Clint said.

"A detective, I know," Fitzgerald said. "His job is to find out who's doing it. His job is not to keep me—and my men—alive."

"I understood there was only property damage."

"So far," Fitzgerald said. "But each case escalates until . . . who knows? Somebody's going to get hurt, Clint. Somebody's going to die."

"So you want me to be . . . what? Security? A bodyguard?"

"I'll announce that you've been hired to be my assistant, my number two. I'll put you on salary."

"And how's the town going to react to that?"

"I don't know," Fitzgerald said. "Let's see. I've got to deal with the mayor, the town council—which is in charge of allocating the twenty-five thousand. I've also had dealings with the sheriff and the chief of police, as well as other prominent citizens."

"Like Patrick Bodeen?"

Fitzgerald looked surprised.

"How do you know about him?"

"I met his wife."

"Christ," Fitzgerald said, "already? I should've known. She approached you, right?"

"Right."

"Yeah, she's poison, Clint. Trouble."

"And what's he do?"

"He's a very prominent rancher, and doesn't like the university being built so close to his property."

"Where did the land come from?"

"There was almost no land," Fitzgerald said. "The

town actually discussed giving the money back, but then two gamblers and one saloon owner stepped and donated the necessary property."

"So do you think Bodeen is responsible for the sabotage?"

"Maybe," Fitzgerald said. "He's got the money to hire it done. But his wife has so much of his attention, keeps him running, I don't see where he'd get the time."

"Anybody else you suspect?"

"A few people, but hey, that's the job of the police. That's not what I want you to do."

"I'm not a night watchman, Fitz."

"I know it. I don't expect you to sit out there at the site with a shotgun."

"Okay," Clint said, "just so we're agreed on that."

"I'll give you a good salary."

"That come out of the twenty-five thousand?"

"No," Fitz said, "I don't think I'd be able to justify that. I'll pay you out of my own pocket."

"Okay," Clint said, "I'll take five dollars a day."

"Five dollars? That's all? Clint, that's hardly—"

"It's enough for beer and steak and some other odds and ends."

"Well, I'll handle the hotel, then. I can put you in a better one—"

"This one's good enough."

"Then it's done?"

"It's done," Clint said. "I'm hired."

The two friends shook hands across the table.

"What do you say we get out of here and get something to eat?" Fitz said.

EIGHT

Patrick Bodeen looked up from his desk as Andrew Leland entered his office.

"Good evening, Sheriff."

"Patrick." Leland walked to the sidebar and poured himself a brandy. He held the glass up to Bodeen, who nodded.

They were in Bodeen's house, about three miles outside of town. Bodeen's property adjoined the property the university was being built on.

Leland handed Bodeen a glass of his own brandy, and sat across from him.

"We got a visitor in town today."

"Is that a fact? And why does that concern me?"

"It's Clint Adams."

"The Gunsmith?" Bodeen sat back in his chair. "What's he want here?"

"Apparently," Leland said, "he's friends with Fitzgerald."

"Did Fitzgerald call him here?"

"He says he stopped in to see his friend," Leland said.

"Just by coincidence?"

Leland shrugged.

"Can't be," Bodeen said. "Fitzgerald must have sent for him."

"A man like that is trouble, no matter how he got here."

"Does the mayor know?"

"I'll bet. His bird dog, Fairman, must have seen him ride in."

"All right," Bodeen said, "thanks for letting me know."

Leland sat where he was and sipped his brandy.

Bodeen opened a drawer in the desk, took out an envelope, and tossed it across the desk. Leland leaned forward, picked it up, and set his empty glass down.

"I'll keep an eye on him, let you know what's going on," he said, standing up.

"You do that. Has he seen Fitzgerald yet?"

"Not when the chief and I saw him," Leland said, "but maybe since then. I don't know. He hasn't been out to the site."

"All right, Andy," Bodeen said, "thanks."

Leland left, and Bodeen sat back in his chair. Moments later, his wife entered the room, wearing a silk nightgown that left little to the imagination. She did this to tease him, he knew, because he hadn't touched her in years.

"What did that little bug want?" she asked.

"It's no concern of yours."

"Really?" she asked. She got herself a glass of brandy, remained standing while she drank it. "Was he here to tell you that Clint Adams is in town?"

He narrowed his eyes.

"How did you know that?"

"I met him."

"When?"

"This afternoon."

"Where?"

"In the restaurant," she said, "after you stormed out like a petulant child."

"Now there's the pot calling the kettle black. What did Mr. Adams have to say to you? Did you fuck him?"

"No, of course not," she said, and then added, "not yet."

"Get out, Cynthia," he said. "I don't have time for you."

She put her glass down and headed out of the room. At the door she turned and said, "But I'll let you know when I do."

NINE

The door to Mayor Darling's office opened and Chief Coleman stuck his head in.

"Your girl's not here," he said.

"Of course not," Darling said. "She keeps regular business hours. Come on in, Chief."

Coleman entered, closed the door behind him, and then seated himself across from the mayor.

"What's on your mind?" the mayor asked.

"The Gunsmith."

"I heard."

"I figured," Coleman said.

"What's he want here?"

"He says he's passing through, stopped in to see a friend."

"And that friend would be . . ."

"Ted Fitzgerald."

Darling laughed sharply, sat back in his chair.

"That figures." The mayor drummed his fingers on the

arms of his chair for a while, then folded them across his belly. "Has he seen Fitzgerald?"

"Not that I know of. They were supposed to meet at six at Adams's hotel, but Fitzgerald never showed up. Of course, they could have met by now."

"Dennis will let me know," Darling said. "He'd better."

"What do you want to do?"

"Nothing," Darling said. "You've still got your man looking into the business at the university. Let's see how this shakes out. Maybe he'll see Fitzgerald and leave town."

"Yes, maybe."

Darling pinched the bridge of his nose with his right thumb and forefinger.

"Did you speak with him?"

"Yes."

"How did that come about?"

"Leland brought him to me."

"How did that happen?"

Coleman explained the circumstances.

Darling laughed. "You have a man working for you who never heard of the Gunsmith?"

"Apparently."

Darling laughed again. It seemed to do him some good. He sat forward in his chair, his elbows on his desk.

"All right, Chief," he said, "thanks for letting me know. Just keep me informed about your investigation."

"Yes, sir."

Coleman left, pulling the door closed behind him. Mayor Darling took a bottle of whiskey from his bottom drawer, pulled directly from it, and then replaced it.

This job was going to kill him.

TEN

"So," Clint said when he and Fitz were seated in a restaurant with bowls of stew in front of them, "tell me who's aligned with who."

"Well, you met both the sheriff and the chief of police," Fitz said. "Coleman reports right to Mayor Darling."

"Darling?"

"That's the least of his problems," Fitz said. "Now Leland, he's aligned with Patrick Bodeen."

"So Bodeen is at odds with the mayor?"

Fitz nodded and said, "That's because Bodeen was mayor before Darling came along and beat him. Now if Bodeen can make Darling look bad, he'll run again and get this office back."

"So he's willing to use the university to make that happen?"

"He'll use anything."

"Including his wife?"

"No," Fitz said, "you've got to understand that relationship. She's the user there."

"Why doesn't he divorce her?"

"The money is hers," Fitz said.

"So why doesn't she divorce him?"

"That's a good question," Fitz said. "Maybe she likes torturing him. Maybe it's easier for her to cat around while she's married."

"Who is she catting around with lately?"

"Don't know," Fitz said. "It seems like she might be taking a break."

"So when she's sleeping around, it's no secret?"

"Nope," Fitz said. "She doesn't care who knows."

"Okay," Clint said, "let's talk about your site. Where do you sleep?"

"I've got a room in town, at the Silver Spur, but we built a shack out there and most of the time Art Sideman and me sleep there."

"Sideman?"

"He's the architect."

"And he's being paid out of the twenty-five thousand?" Clint asked.

Fitz nodded and said, "Same as me."

"Who else is out there?"

"We built a bunkhouse for the construction crew."

"You trust all of them?"

"Hell, no," Fitz said. "They're for hire, like anyone else. If somebody got to them with enough money, I'm sure they'd sabotage the project."

"So you have to keep a close eye on them."

"I have a foreman."

"Trust him?"

"Yes, I've used him before. I'll introduce you to him."

"Anybody wear a gun out there?"

"Steve, the foreman."

"Can he use it?"

"Yeah, he can hit what he aims at. And he's not afraid to use it."

"Well, that's good."

"I don't suppose you'd want to come out and stay in the bunkhouse?"

"I don't think that's good idea," Clint said. "I don't want to make friends with your crew."

Fitz studied him, then smiled and said, "Oh, you want them to stay afraid of you."

"Well, wary anyway," Clint said.

"You could bunk in with Art Sideman and me if you want."

"If it comes to that, okay," Clint said. "The foreman, he bunk with the men?"

"Yeah, he prefers to do it that way. Keeps them in line."

"I'll want to come out tomorrow and look things over."

"That's no problem. I'll stay in town tonight and take you out there."

"I heard it's a straight run east to the main road?" Clint asked.

"That's right. Who told you?"

"Sheriff Leland. In fact, he wanted to take me out there tonight."

"That was very helpful of him."

"He and the chief seem to get along."

"They do," Fitz said. "They were hired at the same

time, and even though they might be on opposite sides, they get along fine."

"That's civil."

"Clint," Fitz said, "I sent for you because I think things are about to get uncivil."

"Well," Clint said, "we'll see what we can do about that."

ELEVEN

After eating, they went to another saloon and had a few beers. They caught up on what they'd each been doing since they last saw each other, and then they split up. Clint said he was going back to his hotel. Fitz said he was going to do the same. Clint had no choice but to believe his friend. If the man had a woman in town, he hadn't said so, but Clint knew Fitz to have the normal attraction to women. Clint felt sure that, by this time, Fitz must have had a woman in town.

But that wasn't his business. He went back to his hotel, stripped down, read for a while—Dickens—and then went to sleep. He was very happy that no one knocked on his door that night.

Fitz ran his hands over the smooth, warm skin of her breasts, tweaked the nipples with his fingers, then leaned over and licked them. She sighed as her nipples became distended.

"I love when they do that," Fitz said.

"Does he know?" Cynthia asked, holding Fitz's head in place.

"Hmm?" he said, his mouth filled with as much of one breast as he could accommodate.

"Your friend, the Gunsmith," she said. "Does he know about us?"

"Oh, no," he said, lifting his head and looking at her. "I didn't tell him a thing. God, you're beautiful."

"Won't he be mad when he finds out?"

"Maybe he won't find out," he said.

She looked at him, her eyes moving over his naked body. He had a hard cock, and he had done the job for her over the past few months, but she was ready to move on.

She pushed him down on his back on the bed, got down between his legs, and holding him in one hand, began to lick him up and down. Finally, she took him in her mouth and began to suck him.

He grunted as her head began to move up and down on him, lifting his hips to meet her. They continued that way until he couldn't hold back any longer, and he erupted . . .

Later, he slid his cock up into her steamy depths and began to fuck her as hard and fast as he could. She gasped and spoke to him, exhorting him on, but in reality she was simply waiting for him to finish. She was just about finished with Ted Fitzgerald, so maybe Clint Adams had come to town just in time.

He continued to rut, and gasp, and snort until he exploded into her.

"That's it, baby," she said in his ear, "give it to me."

He gasped and jerked and finally rolled off her, onto his back.

"I have to go," she said, getting out of bed.

"So soon?"

"I have to get back, Ted," she said. She used a cloth to clean herself, and then got dressed.

"When can I see you again?"

"I'm not sure," she said. "It might be harder with your friend in town."

"I need him here," he said, "but we can work around him."

"We'll have to see," she said. She leaned down and kissed him. He grabbed for her but she danced away, out of his reach. "I'll see you when I see you."

She slipped out the door, closing it gently behind him. He thought about her for a few minutes, but he was exhausted and that was all the time he was able to give to thought.

He fell asleep.

TWELVE

Clint woke the next morning, went downstairs, and met Fitz for breakfast. They ate right in the hotel, then walked to the livery and saddled their horses.

"Wow," Fitz said when he saw Eclipse. "What happened to that other big black you had?"

"Duke? Same thing that happens to all of us. He got old, put out to pasture."

"When are you going to get put out to pasture?"

"Who'll put me out?" Clint asked.

"How about putting yourself out?"

"No," Clint said. "I'm going to die in the saddle, I think. Or at the end of a bullet. But not out in some pasture."

They walked their horses outside and mounted up.

"Okay," Fitz said. "Couple of hours and we'll be there."

"Main road," Clint said.

"Let's hit it."

* * *

They passed other riders, other vehicles, along the road. Each time a hat was tipped, or a wave exchanged. Fitz said he didn't know any of them, but people around here did that.

Finally, up ahead, Clint spotted a partially erected building. Most of it was brick, some of it was wood. It was impressive, but it was still a long way from finished.

They reined in.

"What do you think?"

"It's going to be big."

"Yeah, it is."

"So," Clint said, "the mental institution would have been bigger?"

"Oh, yeah," Fitz said, "bigger, and it would have yielded more jobs."

"And a lot of that money would have lined a lot of pockets."

"Oh, yeah," Fitz said. "That, too."

Fitz led the way to the construction site, and then around it. Two small buildings, which had been hidden by the partially finished one, came into view—the bunkhouse and the shack Fitz slept in.

The construction site was a flurry of activity. There were men on the ground, men up on scaffolding, men on the roof. Watching it all stood a man wearing a gun.

"That's Steve," Fitz said. "Come on, I'll introduce you."

They rode over to the shack and dismounted.

"There's a lean-to behind the bunkhouse. That's where we keep the horses. There are also a couple of buckboards back there."

They walked over to where the foreman was standing, arms folded across his chest.

"Steve!"

Steve Taylor turned. He was in his forties, with a weathered face and big, scarred hands.

"Boss."

"Steve, this is Clint Adams."

"Hey," Steve said, shaking hands. "He said you'd come."

"Well, I hate being predictable."

"You gonna stay and help?"

"Looks like it."

"Good," Taylor said. "I won't be the only gun around here."

"Where's Art?" Fitz asked.

"In the shack, looking over his plans."

"Again?" Fitz looked at Clint. "He does this all the time. Goes over the plans, tries to change some things. I have to rein him in."

"Well, you better do it again," Steve said. "Good to meet you. I gotta go up there. Somebody's wavin'."

Clint looked up, saw a man waving.

"Come on," Fitz said. "I'll introduce you to Art."

They walked over to the shack while Steve Taylor went into the building, presumably to make his way to the roof.

When they opened the door of the shack and walked in, a man turned and looked at them. He'd been standing over a table, looking down. Now he stared at them through thick eyeglasses. He was tall, thin, looked to be all knees and elbows. Clint guessed him to be about forty.

"Ted! I'm glad you're here. Look at this. I figured out a way—"

"Art, settle down," Fitz said, cutting him off. "I want you to meet Clint Adams."

"Oh, hey, glad to meet you," Art Sideman said. "Fitz, I figured out—"

"Art!" Fitz said. "Take a breath. This is the man I told you I was going to ask for help. The Gunsmith."

"Oh!" Sideman looked surprised. His magnified eyes seemed incredibly wide. "You came!"

"I came."

"Well, now maybe we can stop worryin' about fires and vandalism and just concentrate on building this thing!"

"We'll do our best," Fitz said.

"Fitz, I gotta show you this!" Sideman said, pointing to the plans.

"Art—"

"Fitz, go ahead," Clint said. "I'm going to take a walk around the site."

"Well, okay," Fitz said. "I'll talk to you later. Okay, Art, whataya got here?"

Clint left the shack, walked over to the bunkhouse. It was empty, as everyone was either around or on the building. Behind the bunkhouse he found a few team horses, and a couple of buckboards they obviously used to haul building equipment.

He came back around and watched the men work for a while. A few of them threw some glances his way, but they kept working. If they had any curiosity about him, they were waiting to satisfy it.

Finally, Steve Taylor came back down to the ground and walked up to him.

"Anything I can do for you?"

"Heard you had some fires."

"Oh, yeah."

"Can you show me where?"

"Sure, come on."

They walked around to one side of the building. Clint immediately saw the charred wall. He walked up to it, touched it, then sniffed his fingers.

"This was recent," Clint said.

"Last week."

"Were the police out here?"

"Yeah, they sent a detective."

"What did he do?"

"Talked to some of the men, looked around . . . he never did what you just did. What'd you smell?"

"Something that was used to start the fire," Clint said. "Maybe some lamp oil."

"Sonofabitch."

Clint looked around. Anyone intending to sabotage the place would not just ride up to it. They'd leave their horse or wagon a ways off and walk the rest of the way.

"I'm going to ride around for a while, see if I can find where they left their horse, or wagon."

"Want me to come along?"

"No, you've got work to do. I'll be okay. Just tell Fitz where I am."

"I'll tell 'im."

Clint went back to Eclipse, mounted up, and rode off.

THIRTEEN

He drove in an ever-widening circle away from the building until he came upon some tracks. He dismounted, got down on his knee, then walked around a bit. Somebody had been here with a wagon—probably a buckboard—and a horse. Two men, maybe more. Probably came out with a couple of large cans of lamp oil. The mounted man was probably their bodyguard.

The tracks were a week old, and they could still be followed.

Clint mounted up and rode back to the site.

Fitz was standing next to Steve Taylor, watching the men work. When he saw Clint riding back, he said something to his foreman and walked over to meet him.

"Where you been?" Fitz asked.

"Found some tracks," Clint said. "Buckboard and saddle horse."

"How old?"

"About a week."

"That matches the fire," Fitz said. "Can you follow them?"

"I can. I wanted to come back and let you know."

"Want me to come with you?"

"No," Clint said, "I don't know what I'll run into and you don't have a gun."

"Then take Steve," Fitz said. "He can take my horse."

"Okay," Clint said, "I'll take him."

Fitz ran over to Steve. They exchanged a few words, then Steve nodded and walked over to Clint.

"Ready to go?" Clint asked.

"I'm ready," Steve said. "I hope we catch these sonsofbitches."

Steve mounted Fitz's horse and followed Clint.

They rode back to the tracks, which Clint pointed out to Steve.

"Damn," Steve said "I never came out here to look, and neither did the police. I coulda followed those buckboard tracks."

"Well, that's what we're going to do now."

They mounted up and started following the tracks.

They followed the tracks for a few miles, and then suddenly the horse split off from the buckboard.

"Now where's he going?" Taylor asked, pointing at the saddle horse's tracks.

"Well, the buckboard looks like it's circling," Clint said. "It's going to head back to town."

"And the horse?"

"Well, he's going somewhere else."

"But where?"

"Well, that's what we're going to find out," Clint said. "The buckboard's going to town, so we can track that anytime. These other tracks will fade out long before those wheel ruts."

"Why don't we split up?" Taylor asked. "One of us follows the buckboard and the other follows the horse."

"There's no need for that," Clint said. "Those wheel tracks aren't going anywhere. Let's see where the rider is going, and then we can decide what to do."

"Well, okay," Taylor said. "You're in charge."

They turned their horses and started following the tracks of the horse.

An hour later they were on top of a hill, looking down at a ranch.

"Do you know whose ranch that is?"

"I do," Taylor said. "It belongs to Patrick Bodeen."

"Bodeen."

"So he's the one behind the fire."

"Well, not necessarily him," Clint said, "but it is somebody who rode here after the fire."

"You think somebody's tryin' to frame him?"

"I don't know," Clint said, "but I'm going to find out . . . eventually."

"We're not gonna ride down there?"

"Not right now, Steve," Clint said. "I want to go back to the other tracks and follow them."

"So you'll be going back to town."

"Looks like it."

"Okay, then I'll go back to the site," Taylor said. "I've got work to do."

"And you'll tell Fitz where I went?"

"Of course."

Taylor looked down the hill at the Bodeen spread.

"You sure you don't wanna go down there now?"

"I'm sure," Clint said. "I want to be armed with some more information first."

"You gonna tell this to the police?"

"Eventually," Clint said. "I don't want them . . . doing anything before I'm ready."

"Doing anything? Do you mean arresting someone, or warning someone?"

"Either one," Clint said. "Come on. We'll ride back to the buckboard tracks, and then split up there."

"You're the boss."

FOURTEEN

Clint followed the buckboard tracks back toward town, but about a mile outside they took to the main road, which was hard-packed dirt and filled with older ruts. It was obvious the buckboard went back to town, but where it went from there was anyone's guess.

He rode back into town, decided to stay there rather than ride back to the site. Fitz would know where to find him, and now that he had agreed to help, there was somebody he needed to talk with.

He turned Eclipse back over to the liveryman and walked directly to the police station. The same young sergeant was on the desk, and when he looked up, his face colored, but it was more from anger than shame. He was annoyed that he'd been humiliated by Clint.

"Yes, sir?"

"Sergeant, I'd like to see the detective who is investigating the vandalism out at the university building site."

"That would be Detective Fellows, sir," the sergeant

said. "I'm afraid he's not available right now, but I can tell him you'd like to talk to him."

Clint decided not to push it. "Just tell him he can find me at my hotel."

"Yes, sir."

Clint turned and walked out. He went to a nearby small saloon and got himself a beer. He needed to talk to the detective, and to Patrick Bodeen. The tracks leading to his ranch implicated him, though circumstantially. And he thought he should probably talk to the mayor, as well. Might as well do whatever he could do to shake things up with the town fathers. Whatever was going on out at the university site, somebody in the local government had to be involved. No one else would be so upset about Tucson getting the university instead of the mental hospital.

He finished his beer and walked back to his hotel.

"Sir?" the desk clerk called.

"Yes?"

"There was a man here looking for you a little while ago."

"Did he leave his name?"

"No, but he's getting a drink while he waits for you."

Clint looked over at the doorway that led to the saloon.

"What's he look like?"

"Tall, thirties, black hair, he's wearing an Eastern suit and a bowler hat. Oh yeah, and he's got a badge."

"Thanks."

Clint entered the saloon and looked around. The fact that the place was not popular with the locals made the man easy to pick out. He was seated at a table, nursing a beer. Clint walked over.

"I'm going to guess that you're Detective Fellows."

The man looked up at him and said, "That's right. And you're Mr. Adams?"

"I am."

"Please, have a seat," Fellows said. "Can I get you a beer?"

"That'd be fine, but I'll go to the bar and get it. The service here is terrible."

"Nonsense," Fellows said, standing up. "I'll get it, you sit down."

Clint sat while the detective went to the bar and came back with two beers, another for him despite the fact that his first one was still half full.

"I was just over at the police station looking for you," Clint said.

"Is that a fact?" Fellows asked. "The chief just told me about you today, and I thought we should talk."

The detective was wearing his bowler hat, but he took it off, revealing a receding hairline, despite the fact he was only in his thirties.

"What is your purpose for being in Tucson, Mr. Adams?" he asked.

"I'm friends with Ted Fitzgerald, and I'm determined to see that he's not injured."

"What makes you believe he's in danger of being injured?"

"From what I understand, the vandalism out at the building site seems to be escalating. Somebody's bound to get hurt eventually. I don't want it to be my friend."

"Seems to me your friend has other worries as far as getting hurt."

"What's that mean?"

"Ask him," Fellows said. "Talk to him about Cynthia Bodeen."

"I understood her husband doesn't care who she sleeps with."

"But there are other men who do care," Fellows said. "She's left quite a string of ex-lovers behind her, and they didn't all go away willingly."

Clint tried to keep his reaction off his face. Fitz had told him about Cynthia, but had not mentioned that he was one of her lovers—and in fact, the current one.

"What have you been able to find out so far about the vandalism, Detective?"

"Not much," Fellows said. "I'm still interviewing the workers."

"You think one of the workers did it?"

"I think it's possible that not all the workers are there for the benefit of the construction."

"I see."

"But I have no evidence against any of them."

"I was out there today, rode around some, found some tracks."

"Tracks?"

Clint explained about the two sets of tracks, buckboard and saddle horse.

"I didn't see that," Fellow said, frowning. "Tracking is not one of my strong points. I didn't get to do a lot of that in Philadelphia. Tell me more."

Clint told him about following the tracks, and where they led.

"Once the buckboard hit town, the tracks blended in with the tracks from all the regular traffic."

"And the horse tracks led to Mr. Bodeen's ranch?"

"That's right."

"Have you been out there to talk to him?"

"Not yet."

"If you don't mind, I'd like to go out there with you," Fellows said.

"Suits me," Clint said. "He won't be able to refuse to talk to me, then. But I've got a question for you before we go out there, Detective."

"What's that, sir?"

"Are you one of the ex-lovers who didn't go away willingly?"

Fellows actually smiled with such amusement that Clint totally believed his next words.

"I'm afraid I'm a little below Mrs. Bodeen's station, Mr. Adams, which suits me just fine. I don't need the extra headache while I'm trying to establish myself here in Tucson."

The detective sounded like quite a smart young man.

FIFTEEN

Clint was surprised that Detective Fellows wanted to go out to Bodeen's place immediately.

"Why not?" Fellows asked. "There's still plenty of light, so why wait?"

"I'll saddle my horse," Clint said.

"I'll be taking a buggy," Fellows said. "I'm not much of a horseman. Would you like to ride with me?"

"I think I'd prefer to take my horse."

"Fine. Meet you out in front of your hotel."

They left the hotel together and split up. Clint went back to the livery to collect Eclipse for the second time that day.

Sitting in his buggy in front of the hotel, Fellows looked more like a country doctor ready to go out to make his calls rather than a detective going out to conduct an investigation. In fact, he even had a leather bag on the seat that looked like a doctor's bag.

"What's in the bag?" Clint asked, riding up alongside him.

"Tools that I use to collect evidence," Fellows said. "Ready to go?"

"Let's ride," Clint said.

When they reached the Bodeen place, Clint took Fellows to show him the tracks.

"How can you tell these tracks from other horses?" the detective asked.

"See there? There's a nick on the horseshoe of the rear left foot. That'll stand out from other horseshoes."

"Like fingerprints."

"I've heard of that," Clint said. "In fact, Mark Twain used them in a couple of his books, *Life on the Mississippi* and *Pudd'nhead Wilson*."

"The British first began using them in eighteen fifty-eight," Fellows said. "But I find this very interesting. If I had some water, I could take a plaster cast of this hoofprint."

"We can come back out and do that later," Clint said. Why don't we ride up to the house now and see how Mr. Bodeen reacts."

"I'm with you."

As they pulled up in front of the house, several hands drifted over from the corral and barn to greet them. The tracks they were following had disappeared among all the other tracks on the ground. They couldn't tell if they led to the house, or the barn, or anywhere else.

"Gentlemen," Fellows said, "I'm Detective Fellows from the Tucson Police Department. I need to see your boss."

"That'd be Doug Melvin," one of them said.

"Who?" Fellows asked.

"The foreman," another man said.

"I meant that I wish to see Mr. Bodeen."

"Well, you'll have to go through the foreman first," somebody else said.

"And where would he be?" Fellows asked.

"He's in the barn," another man said.

"We'll walk ya over."

Fellows got down from his buggy and Clint dismounted and dropped Eclipse's reins to the ground.

"That's a fine-lookin' horse, mister," one man said.

"Yeah, he is."

"You sure you don't wanna tie him off?" another voice called.

"He's fine where he is," Clint said. "I wouldn't advise anybody to get to close to him, though. He bites."

"Lead the way," Fellows said to the men.

They not only led the way, but surrounded Clint and Fellows and walked them over to the barn that way.

One man entered the barn, yelling, "Hey, boss, there's a lawman out here ta see ya!"

"What the hell do I want to see a lawman for?" another voice bellowed.

The foreman appeared, a big, burly man who wore a gun, but looked as if he settled most disputes with his fists.

"Who's the lawman?" he asked.

"That would be me," Fellows said. "Detective Fellows."

Doug Melvin pinned Clint with a hard stare and asked, "And who are you?"

"Clint Adams."

A stir went through the assembled ranch hands.

"Okay, the rest of you get back to work!" Melvin shouted. "Now."

Slowly, the men drifted away.

"Don't wanna get the men too excited," Melvin said. "What's the Gunsmith want here?"

"I'm just riding with him," Clint said, indicating Fellows. "He's in charge."

"That a fact?"

"It is," Fellows asked. "And I'm not here to see you. want to see Mr. Bodeen."

"What about?"

"That's private," Fellows said. "I would think if he wants you to know, he'd tell you after we leave."

Melvin stared at Fellows for a few moments, then said, "Lemme see your badge."

Fellows took it out and showed it to him. It was silver, and said TUCSON POLICE on it, but it wasn't shaped as a star.

"Pretty fancy," Melvin said, handing it back. "Me, I prefer sheriffs and marshals."

"So do I," Clint said.

"Yeah," Melvin said. "you would."

"Mr. Melvin, I'm going to have to insist on seeing your boss."

"Yeah, okay," Melvin said. "Walk with me to the house. You'll have to wait on the porch while I go inside."

"Very well."

The foreman led them back to the house, up the steps to the porch, then left them there and went inside.

"Think he'll try to turn us away?" Clint asked.

"I doubt it," Fellows said. "He's a prominent citizen, he'll want to appear cooperative."

"You think?"

"Why would he not?"

"Because," Clint said, "he's a prominent citizen. In my opinion, such men like to flex their muscles."

The front door opened and the foreman stuck his head out.

"Gents? The boss says he'll see you."

Fellows gave Clint a look and they followed the foreman inside.

SIXTEEN

Clint expected the foreman to lead them to an office. Instead, he led them through the house and out through some glass doors. In the back was a section of ground covered with what appeared to be pieces of slate. There was a table, and some chairs. A man he assumed was Patrick Bodeen was standing by the table, holding a large drink.

"Mr. Bodeen?" the foreman said. "This here's Detective Fellows, and that other fella is Clint Adams."

"All right, Doug," Bodeen said. "Thanks. You can go."

"Yes, sir."

Bodeen approached both men with a proffered hand. He was tall, slender, gray-haired with a widow's peak. Although he was supposedly in his own house drinking alone, his suit was very expensive. Clint looked at the table. Although there was no glass there, there was a wet circle where a glass had been. The question was, Bodeen's glass or someone else's?

"Good to meet you both," he said. "Mr. Adams, I know your reputation, of course."

"Glad to meet you, Mr. Bodeen," Clint said.

"Can I get either of you a drink?" Bodeen asked, lifting the glass in his left hand.

"Not for me, thanks," Clint said.

"Nor me," Fellows said.

"Very well," Bodeen said, "I suppose we should get down to business. What can I do for you gents?"

All three men remained standing, which seemed to set the tone of the meeting.

"I'm sure you've heard about the vandalism that's been taking place out at the site of the new university?" Fellows asked.

"Of course," Bodeen said. "I know what's going on in the area."

"Well, we found some tracks leading from the building site to here."

"Here? Here where?"

"Your ranch."

"I mean, exactly where?"

"Once the tracks reach the general area, they get swallowed up by other tracks," Clint said. "They could lead right to your barn, though."

"Could," Bodeen said, "but you have no proof of that."

"We do know the rider came here," Fellows said.

"And you think that means . . . what? That he's working here? For me? Suppose the man rode here and was turned away?"

"Did such a man come here, and did you turn him away?" Fellows asked.

"Did he come here when? What was the exact day?

No, never mind. I won't remember where I was anyway. Just tell me why you're really here. Do you think I've been having the university site vandalized?"

"I'm not saying that, sir," Fellows said. "I'm just asking questions."

"You're just asking questions of a prominent Tucson citizen, Fellows," Bodeen said. "I'm not without influence in this town—or this state, for that matter. You could be in a lot of trouble."

"For doing my job, sir?" Fellows asked. "Why would I be in trouble for that?"

Bodeen glared at Fellows, but before he could bluster any further, Clint asked, "Where's your wife, Mr. Bodeen?"

"What?" Bodeen switched his glare from Fellows to Clint. "What do you mean?"

"I'm just wondering if she's home."

"What's that got to do with anything?"

"I was just wondering," Clint said. "I thought she might have been out here having a drink with you."

He walked to the table, and with his forefinger obliterated the wet circle left by a glass.

"If you knew anything about me, Mr. Adams," Bodeen said, "you'd know that I don't usually drink with my wife. In fact, we rarely speak."

"Well," Clint said, "I was just wondering."

"In fact," Bodeen said, "you've met my wife, haven't you?"

"Now that you mention it, yes, we have met," Clint said.

"In fact," Bodeen said, "for all I know, you've slept with the whore. Everyone else seems to have."

"Not me," Clint said.

"Nor me," Fellows said.

That remark seemed to amuse Patrick Bodeen.

"Gents," he said, "if that's all, I have things to do."

"I'd like to take a look at the horses in your stable, Mr. Bodeen," Fellows said.

"I don't think I'm going to be that cooperative, Detective."

"I can get an order from the court," Fellows said.

"You do that," Bodeen said. "When you have it, come back and we'll see what we can do. Now, I think you gentlemen can show yourselves out. Be assured I'll be talking to the chief, and to the mayor, about this."

"That doesn't mean much to me, Mr. Bodeen," Clint said. "If you have anything to do with vandalizing the university, I'll find out."

"You do that, Mr. Adams," Bodeen said. "Just remember, I have all kinds of friends, from every walk of life."

"Is that a threat?"

"No, Mr. Adams," Bodeen said, "that's a suggestion."

Clint looked at Fellows, who shrugged, and the two men went back into the house.

When they came out the front door, they found the foreman, Melvin, standing by their horses.

"What the hell is wrong with this horse of yours, Adams?" he demanded. "He nearly bit off one of my men's fingers."

"I warned them," Clint said.

"Did you get what you wanted from the boss?" Melvin asked.

"Pretty much," Clint said.

"We'll be back," Fellows said.

He got into his buggy, Clint mounted up, and they rode out.

SEVENTEEN

When the ranch was behind them and out of sight, Fellows reined his horse in, and Clint followed his lead.

"What do you think?" he asked Clint.

"He's hiding something."

"That horse with the distinctive print might be in that barn."

"Well," Clint said, "if it is, it won't be for long."

"I need to get back to town and talk to my chief, and a judge."

"You think a judge will give you what you need?" Clint asked. "Against Patrick Bodeen?"

Fellows looked crestfallen.

"Probably not."

"In the time it takes you go back to town and find that out," Clint said, "they could get rid of that horse, or reshoe it."

"You're not suggesting we sneak back there and have a look, are you?"

"No."

"Good," Fellows said with some relief.

"I'm suggesting we sneak back and have a look . . . after dark!"

They had hours to kill, but didn't want to go too far away. It took Clint a while to convince Fellows they were doing the right thing.

"This isn't back East, Fellows," he said. "You can't just run to a judge and get what you want."

They found a copse of trees that would hide the buggy and the horses well enough. Then they crept back to within sight of the ranch to watch until dark.

"What can we do from here if they decide to get rid of that horse?" Fellows asked.

"Not much," Clint said. "You'd just have to swear you saw them moving it."

"But if they bring a horse out, we can't assume it's the right one."

"No, we can't."

"We'd have to try to take it from them."

"Let's just wait and see what happens, Fellows."

"Fred," Fellows said.

"What?"

"My name's Fred."

"Fred Fellows?"

The detective looked at him. "What's wrong with that?"

"Nothing," Clint said. "It's very . . . catchy."

They watched for a couple of hours, and then it started to get dark.

"Let's go," Clint said.

"Now? It's not dark yet."

"It will be by the time we work our way down behind the barn."

He slapped the younger man on the back and led the way down to the barn. By the time they had their backs pressed against the back wall, darkness had fallen.

"You want to call this?" Clint asked.

"I'm still new out here," Fellows said, "and you have the experience. I'll follow you, Mr. Adams."

"Clint," he said. "Just call me Clint."

"All right."

"We'll go in, and you watch the front door while I check the horses."

"And if the horse is there?" Fellows asked.

"Then we need to find out who it belongs to."

"And if it's not here?"

"Then we have to try something else," Clint said. "That would mean either they succeeded in hiding it, or we're wrong."

"I don't think we're wrong," Fellows said. "I saw the trail, plain as day."

"No, I don't think we're wrong either," Clint said, "but we'll see."

Clint led the way along one side of the barn, the side that was hidden from the house. When he got to the front, he peered around, made sure they were clear, and then entered the barn.

Immediately, he knew they had a problem. He heard somebody moving around, then saw the man working some hay with a pitchfork.

Clint turned to Fellows, put his finger to his lips, and then crept farther into the barn.

He came up behind the ranch hand who was holding the pitch fork.

"Just stand easy," he said aloud. "Don't make any sudden moves."

The man froze.

EIGHTEEN

They tied the man up, gagged him, and stuck him in a corner.

"Just sit quiet and you'll be fine," Clint said, tapping the man on the head.

The man's eyes were wide with fear, but he gave a quick jerky nod of his head.

Clint turned to Fellows and said, "Okay, keep watch at the door."

Fellows nodded and positioned himself there.

Bodeen's ranch was a big one, and the barn was huge. With many stalls, all of which were occupied by horses. He started going to them, one by one, lifting their rear left hooves and checking the shoe there.

As he neared the last of the horses, he began to fear they were too late. Somehow, they had managed to reshoe the horse, or get it out of here.

He lifted the last hoof, then lifted the others. It seemed clear the horse had three old shoes and one new one.

"Fred!"

Fellows looked up, then trotted over to where Clint was standing.

"Is that it?"

"I think so," Clint said. "See here?"

"That shoe looks new."

"Not so much the shoe as the nails," Clint said, "but you're right."

"So who's horse is it?" Fellows asked.

"That's what we have to find out next."

"We can go to the house and ask."

"We can do better than that," Clint said. "We can ask our friend here."

They walked to the trussed-up ranch hand and Clint leaned over him.

"I'm going to remove your gag," he told the man. "If you try to yell, I'll kill you. Understand?"

The man nodded. Clint slipped the gag from his mouth.

"Now I'm going to stand you up."

"Okay."

Clint and Fellows got the man to his feet.

"See that horse?" Clint asked, pointing.

"Y-Yessir."

"Do you know who it belongs to?"

"Y-Yes."

Clint waited, then snapped, "Well, who?"

"T-That mare belongs to Mrs. Bodeen."

Clint looked at Fellows.

"Bodeen's wife?" Fellows asked. "She set the fire at the site?"

"I doubt it," Clint said, "but maybe she let somebody use her horse."

"So we go and ask her."

"Yes," Clint said, "but not now. Not here."

"Then where? When?"

"In town," Clint said, "away from here. There are too many men here."

He turned, put his hand against the bound man's chest, and knocked him over.

"Let's go."

"We're leaving him here?"

"He didn't do anything," Clint said. "He was just doing his job."

"But he'll tell Bodeen we were here."

"That's fine," Clint said. "You told him you'd be investigating."

"So . . . what do we do?"

Clint looked at Fellows and said, "Let's go and get something to eat. I'm starving."

NINETEEN

When they got back to Tucson, they went for thick, juicy steaks.

"As soon as Bodeen finds out what we did, he'll come to town," Fellows said. "He'll talk to Chief Coleman and to Mayor Darling."

"And then what?"

"And then I'll probably get fired."

"Will you quit, then?"

"Quit . . . what? If I'm fired, I won't have a job."

"So you'll stop investigating?"

"Why would I continue?" Fellows asked. "A job is a job."

"Well," Clint said, "it's not a job to me. I'll continue and find out who's been doing damage to the site, before they hurt . . . or kill someone."

"You think they mean to kill someone?"

"Maybe not," Clint said. "But in my experience, these kinds of actions usually lead to it."

"Well," Fellows said around a hunk of meat, "I suppose if it comes to that, I could probably still help you."

"If you get fired," Clint said, "it may not happen."

"I suppose."

They ordered more beer and continued to eat.

"We found Bailey in the barn, trussed up like a pig,"
Doug Melvin told Bodeen.

"And? What does he have to say for himself?"

"He says two men tied him up and then looked at all
the horses."

"And?"

"When they found something, they asked him whose
horse it was."

"And whose horse was it?" Bodeen asked.

"Uh, it was Mrs. Bodeen's mare, sir."

"And what did they find?"

"He doesn't know," Melvin said. "He says they looked
at all the horses' rear hooves."

"I see."

Bodeen sat back in his chair. He was holding a glass
of whiskey in his hand.

"Where is she?"

"I don't know."

"Probably in somebody's bed," Bodeen said.

"Sir . . . can I ask a question?"

"Sure, Doug," Bodeen said. "You're probably the only
person I can trust."

"Thank you. I, uh, was just wondering why you put up
with her. Why don't you just . . ."

"Kill her?"

"No," Melvin said, "but get rid of her."

"Tell me something, Doug."

"What?"

"Why have you never slept with my wife?"

"Because," Melvin said, "I'm the only one you trust."

"All right," Bodeen said, "have my horse brought around in the morning."

"Don't you want to know who Bailey said tied him up?" Melvin asked.

"Oh, I already know," Bodeen said. "I'll be riding into town in the morning to take care of them."

"Yes, sir."

"And you will be coming with me."

"I'll be ready," Melvin said. "See you then, sir."

"Good night, Doug."

"I have a room at the Crystal," Fellows said. "I guess I might have to give that up, too, if I get fired."

They were walking down the almost deserted Tucson main street. The only sound came from the various saloons and dance halls.

"I'm sure there are rooms at my hotel," Clint said, "but why worry about it before it happens?"

"You're probably right," Fellows said. "I'll just go to work in the morning and see what happens."

"Good man," Clint said. "I'll be at my hotel, and I'll probably have breakfast there. If you want to join me, come by."

"I might do that," Fred Fellows said. "Thank you, Clint."

"For what?"

"It was an interesting day, no matter what happens."

Clint slapped the man on the back and said, "I'll see you in the morning."

"Good night."

Clint watched the younger man walk off into the darkness, then turned and walked to his own hotel.

TWENTY

"He wants me to ride into town with him tomorrow," Doug Melvin said.

Cynthia rolled over in bed and looked at him. He looked at her naked ass, reached out, and stroked it.

"So ride in," she said. "He's probably going to try to flex his muscles, get somebody fired. That's about all he can do."

Doug Melvin looked over at the locked door to her room.

"Are you sure he won't come walkin' in here?" he asked.

"He wouldn't dare," she said, "and he's got no reason to."

She kissed his chest, his belly, and moved lower, running her tongue over his penis. It had taken her a while to lure Melvin into her bed, but tonight was the night. She wondered why, but did not hesitate to give it much more thought. She opened her mouth and took his hard cock inside. This was her biggest victory over her husband. His trusted foreman in her power.

Men were so easy, and so stupid . . . but sometimes very tasty.

"So what happened in the barn?" she asked later.

Exhausted, lying on his back, he said, "Two men got in there and inspected all the horses."

"What two men?"

"Clint Adams, and a detective from the police department, somebody named Fellows."

"What were they looking for?"

"My man says they were inspecting the horses' hooves," he told her.

"And why would they do that?"

"My best guess is, they were trying to match a horse's hoof to a track."

"Did they find what they were looking for?" she asked him.

"Maybe," he said. "Bailey said they picked out a certain horse and had him identify the owner."

"And whose horse was it?"

He turned his head and looked at her.

"You really want to know?"

"Yes!" she said. "I asked, didn't I?"

"It was your horse, Cynthia," he said. "Tell me, have you been setting any fires lately?"

"Don't be ridiculous. Did you tell Patrick about this?"

"I did. He's my boss, after all."

She pulled the sheet over her. "You have to leave now, Doug. I want to get some sleep."

"All right," he said.

He got up and got dressed, tried to kiss her but she turned away. He wondered, when the guilt hit him, if this had been worth it.

Cynthia was worried. She had made sure to change the shoe on her horse when she found out about the nick. She didn't really think anyone would be looking closer than that, but then she hadn't expected the Gunsmith to be involved. A man like him would know when a new shoe was put on a horse, even if it didn't look new.

Damn it.

She didn't have much choice. She was going to have to go downstairs and talk to her husband about this. She pulled on one of her heavier robes and went downstairs.

TWENTY-ONE

Clint woke the next morning, hungry. In fact, he was still hungry even though he and Fellows had eaten a big meal when they got back the night before. This morning would be a steak-and-eggs and flapjacks morning.

He went downstairs, didn't find Fred Fellows waiting for him, so he ate alone, then went outside. He had to catch Cynthia Bodeen in town, and alone, so he could ask her about her horse. He sat there in a chair, giving the matter some thought.

Patrick Bodeen came out of the house the next morning, found Doug Melvin waiting with two saddled horses.

"Mornin', boss," the foreman said, fighting off the guilt from having slept with his boss's wife.

"Yeah, good morning," Bodeen said, mounting up.

"Somethin' wrong?"

They started riding toward town together.

"You know what that bitch told me last night?"

"Your wife?"

"What other bitch do I have around? Yes, my wife."

"What'd she say?"

"She replaced the horse shoe on her horse. You know, that hinky one in the back?"

"And?"

"I told her to get rid of the whole horse!" Bodeen said. "Now I have to deal with it."

"Ain't that what we're goin' to town to do today?" Melvin asked.

"Yes," Bodeen said, "that's what we're going to town to deal with today, but Jesus. The bitch could be a little help, couldn't she? Christ!"

Fred Fellows walked into the police station the next morning, ready for the worst. Nobody said a word to him as he walked to his desk. Then he realized it was probably too early—Patrick Bodeen had probably not even been to town yet.

But then a fellow policeman stopped by his desk and said, "The chief wants to see you, Fred."

"When?"

"Now."

"Okay."

Maybe Bodeen had ridden into town early, after all.

Fellows entered the chief's office and Coleman said, "Have a seat, Fred."

"Yessir."

"I want to know where you are with the university vandalism."

"Well, sir, we went out to Mr. Bodeen's ranch and talked to him yesterday."

" 'We'?" Coleman asked. "What do you mean 'we'? Who went with you?"

"Um, Clint Adams was actually going to ride out there himself, so I went along with him to make sure nothing happened."

"What did you think would happen?"

"I don't know, sir," Fellows said, "I was just trying to keep a lid on things, since Mr. Bodeen is such an influential citizen."

"Yes, well, that may have been the right thing to do," the chief said. "What happened?"

"I should back up a bit," Fellows said. "First we rode out to the site and Mr. Adams showed me these tracks he'd found."

"What tracks?"

"Buckboard tracks, and some tracks made by a saddle horse. The buckboard tracks led back here to town, while the other tracks went directly to the Bodeen ranch."

"So that's why you went to the ranch?"

"Yes."

"Did you ask him about the horse?"

"We told him we tracked the horse to his ranch, but he was very uncooperative."

"So you didn't find out who owned the horse?"

"We did, actually."

"Well, who's was it?"

"Um, the horse belonged to Mrs. Bodeen."

"What?"

"It was his wife's horse."

Coleman covered his face with his hands. He wasn't yet secure enough in his job to be able to go up against a man like Patrick Bodeen. He would have to go to the mayor with this.

"All right, anything else?" Coleman asked. "Am I going to hear from Mr. Bodeen about anything?"

"Well . . ."

"What did you do, Detective?" Coleman asked. "Or should I ask what did you and Clint Adams do?"

"We didn't want to leave without finding out whose horse we had followed to the ranch, so we waited until after dark and went in."

"So you went into the man's barn without permission?" the chief asked.

"Yes, sir."

"Keep going, Detective," Chief Coleman said. "Tell me all of it."

Fellows told his boss about tying up one of Bodeen's men and inspecting all the horses. By the time he was done, Chief Coleman did not look very happy.

"You know I'm going to hear about this, Detective," Coleman said.

"Yes, sir."

"Is this the way you conducted your investigations back East?"

"No, sir."

"So you let Clint Adams talk you into this course of action?"

Fellows considered dropping this on Adams and letting him take the responsibility, but in the end he couldn't do it.

"No, sir, I can't say that. I was the one with the badge, so the call was mine."

"So you're willing to take responsibility for this, Detective?"

"Yes, sir."

"All right," Coleman said. "You can go—and try to stay out of trouble, but keep investigating."

"Yes, sir."

As Fred Fellows left the office, Chief Coleman wondered if he was going to end up having to fire him.

Bodeen and his foreman rode into town while Fellows was sitting with his chief.

"Where to first, boss?" Melvin asked.

"The mayor's office," Bodeen said. "I'm going to drop this right in his honor's lap and let him handle it."

"What do you want him to do?"

"Either fire that detective," Bodeen said, "or fire the chief."

"What about Adams?"

"I'll figure out a way to handle the Gunsmith, Doug. Believe me."

"I hope so, boss," Melvin said, "because there he is."

TWENTY-TWO

Clint was still seated outside the hotel when Bodeen and Melvin came riding into town. He held his position, decided to let them see him. They rode by and stared at him, but didn't stop and didn't say anything.

They weren't going to the police station, because they had already passed it, so Clint's guess was Bodeen was going directly to the mayor. He hoped he hadn't gotten the young detective fired.

He turned his head and—speak of the devil—Fred Fellows was walking up to him.

"Mornin', Clint."

"Fred," Clint said. "Are you still employed?"

Fellows stepped up onto the boardwalk and said, "For now."

"You see Bodeen just ride in?"

"That's why I said 'For now,' " Fellows said. "Bodeen and his foreman look like they're riding to the mayor's office."

"That's what I figured."

"What are your plans for today?" Fellows asked.

"I'm going to ride back out to the site to see Fitz and tell him what we found out."

"What did we find out?" Fellows asked.

"Well, the horse that left the tracks belonged to Mrs. Bodeen. That doesn't mean she was riding it at the time, but it does mean that Bodeen's involved."

"So he's been hiring someone to vandalize the university?"

"That would be my guess, unless . . ."

"Unless what?"

"Unless it's Cynthia Bodeen who's been hiring someone to do it," Clint said.

"The woman?"

Clint shrugged.

"Why would she want to sabotage the project?" Fellows asked.

"I don't know," Clint said. "I guess I'll ask her, when I ask her about the horse."

"And when would that be?"

"I'd have to get her alone," Clint said. "Either out at the house, or here in town."

"Well," Fellows said, "Bodeen is in town."

"That's true." Clint got out of his chair. "We could ride out there first, talk to her, then hit the site on the way back. What do you say?"

"Let's do it," Fellows said, "while I still have a badge."

They headed for the livery together.

The mayor's girl stuck her head in his office and said, "Mr. Bodeen's here."

Mayor Darling sat back in his chair and exhaled a big gust of air.

"All right, send him in."

Bodeen came walking in, and the mayor knew the man wasn't happy. All that remained to find out was how much weight he was going to try to throw around.

"Patrick," the mayor said, "what can I do for you this morning?"

"I'll tell you what you can do, David," Bodeen said. He sat across from the mayor and told him what had happened the day and night before.

"What did they find?" he asked when Bodeen was done.

"It doesn't matter what they found," Bodeen said. "They assaulted one of my men."

"What do you want done?"

"I want Adams arrested," Bodeen said, "and I want either the detective or the chief fired."

"I'll have to talk to the chief before I do anything, Patrick," he said. "I mean, if I fire them both, who'll arrest Adams?"

"This isn't funny, Mayor," Bodeen said. "You're trying to find out who's vandalizing your university site, and your police are wasting time with me."

"All right, Patrick," Darling said. "I'll see what I can do."

Bodeen stood up and pointed a finger at the mayor.

"Get it done, Mr. Mayor," he said, "or I'll be looking for your head next."

Darling stood up.

"You're an important man in this county, Patrick, but don't threaten me. I won't stand for it."

"Is that right? We'll see about that."

Bodeen turned and stalked out of the mayor's office. Darling sat back down and exhaled heavily again.

His girl came in and said, "Sir?"

"Get Dennis for me, Mary."

"Yes, sir."

She closed the door, and Darling reclined in his chair. He knew Adams was going to be trouble.

TWENTY-THREE

Clint and Fellows saddled their horses and rode out to the Bodeen ranch as fast as the detective's horse would go. Clint could have outdistanced him with Eclipse, but chose to ride at the detective's pace.

When they arrived at the ranch, they rode up to the house and dismounted. Fellows waved off the ranch hand as they went up the steps.

"We're here to see Mrs. Bodeen," he told them.

"But the boss ain't—" one of them started, but they ignored him and went into the house.

In the house they stopped and Clint shouted, "Cynthia! Are you here?"

They were about to leave the entry foyer to look for her when she appeared at the top of the stairs.

"What the hell are you doing in my house?" she demanded.

"Show her your badge, Fred," Clint suggested.

Fellows took it out and said, "Detective Fellows, ma'am, Tucson Police."

"Not for much longer, Detective, when my husband finds out you burst into our house without permission."

"Sorry, Cynthia, that was my doing."

"Really? Then maybe I should have the detective, here, arrest you."

"Come on down, Cynthia," Clint said. "We need to talk with you."

She started down the steps, but said, "About what?"

"Your horse."

She got to the bottom of the steps and asked, "Would either of you like a drink?"

"No, thanks," Clint said.

"Not me," Fellows said.

"Well, I want one," she said. "You might as well come into the living room."

She didn't wait for them to comment. She started walking, and they followed her.

In the living room she poured herself a brandy from a sidebar, then turned to face them.

"So what's wrong with my horse?"

"It has a new shoe on that doesn't match the others," Clint said.

"I wasn't aware that horseshoes were required to match."

"I think you know what I'm talking about, Cynthia," Clint said.

"I don't think I do, Clint. Why don't you explain it to me?"

"We followed some tracks from the site of a fire at the university," Clint said. "They led us here."

"How does that make it my horse?"

"The track had a distinctive print because of one of

the horseshoes," Clint said, "and you have a new shoe on your horse."

"I don't do the shoeing, Clint," Cynthia said. "That's somebody else's job. If someone reshoed my horse, I don't know anything about it. Why don't you question the men?"

"Does that mean we have permission to question them?" Fellows asked.

"Do you need permission?" she asked.

"Yes, ma'am."

"Then you don't have it. Anything else?"

"Cynthia," Clint said, "what do you have to do with the vandalism out at the university site?"

"Well," she said, "right to the point, Mr. Gunsmith."

"I hope you'll answer me the same way."

"I can do that." She walked up to him so that she was only inches from him, then put her face right close to his. "I don't have anything to do with it."

"Does your husband?' Fellows asked.

"That would be his business," she said. "I don't know anything about my husband's business." She glanced over at Fred, then looked back, staring directly at Clint. "Why don't you get rid of him, and you and I can get better acquainted."

That remark seemed to embarrass Fellows, which both Clint and Cynthia found amusing.

"Look at the young detective," she said. "He's blushing."

"I don't have time today, Cynthia," Clint replied. "Maybe another time."

"Soon, I hope." She backed up, though not very far. "Anything else I can do for you gentlemen?"

"Your husband is in town," Clint said. "I think he

might be trying to get Detective Fellows fired. I would like that not to happen."

"You don't want me to tell him you were here," she said. "You're trying to protect your shy little friend."

"Yes."

"But some of the men must have seen you ride up."

"That's okay," Clint said. "If you don't say anything about it—"

"All right," she said. "I'll do it."

"But?" Clint asked.

"You'll owe me," she said, "and eventually, I'll collect. But you won't know when."

"All right, Cynthia," Clint said.

"Then we have a deal," she said. "You're safe, Mr. Detective."

"Thank you, Mrs. Bodeen."

"Oh, honey," she said, "you can call me Cynthia."

"All right . . . Cynthia."

"And now, boys," she said, "I think you better leave before the man of the house comes back."

"I think you're right," Clint said. "Come on, Fred."

Outside they mounted up and Fellows asked, "What did we find out from that?"

"We found out," Clint said, "that Mrs. Bodeen is a very calm customer."

"But we still don't know if she's involved."

"No, that's right," Clint said. "We don't."

"Then I'm still lost."

"Let's ride out to the site and see what's going on there," Clint suggested.

"Fine," a frustrated Fellows said.

TWENTY-FOUR

When they got to the site, not much had changed. There were still men on the ground, on the walls, and on the roof.

They rode over to the shack where they expected to find Fitz and his architect, Art Sideman. Clint assumed Steve Taylor, the foreman, was somewhere in or near the building with his men.

They walked to the door and opened it. Inside it was as if they had never left. Sideman and Fitz were standing over the plans for the building.

"Well, where have you been?" Fitz asked.

"Fitz, do you know Detective Fellows?" Clint asked.

"Yeah, we've met," Fitz said.

"And this is Art Sideman, the architect," Clint said. "This is Detective Fellows."

"Hello," Sideman said, obviously anxious to get back to his plans.

"What's goin' on? Why are the police here?" Fitz asked.

"Fellows and I have been working together," Clint said. "Did Taylor tell you about the tracks we found?"

"Yeah, he did," Fitz said. "He said you followed one set of tracks to the Bodeen place."

"That's right. And one set to town."

"So what happened? You disappeared."

"I met Fellows and we decided to go out to Bodeen's. If you've got time, we'll tell you about it."

"Fitz, we gotta go over these plans."

"Still going over plans?" Clint asked.

"Art, I gotta take a break." There was another room in the shack. Clint could see two cots in there, but Fitz went in and came out with a bottle of whiskey.

"Come on," Fitz said to Clint. "Bring your policeman."

"I think I'll stay in here and talk to Mr. Sideman," Fellows said.

"Okay," Clint said.

He and Fitz stepped outside. Fitz took the stopper out of the bottle and took a drink, then passed the bottle to Clint, who just took a sip. He told Fitz everything he and Fellows had done and found out.

"Are you tellin' me that Cynthia might be the Bodeen who's causing all this?"

"Well, I considered that for a while," Clint said, "until we spoke to her."

"Now you don't think so?"

"No, she's too calm," Clint said.

"Well, if the horse led you to the ranch, and it's not her, then it's him. And she hates him. Maybe she'll give him up."

"Maybe she will," Clint said. "I get the feeling I'll have the chance to ask her."

"What's that mean?"

"It means I think she'll be coming for me soon," Clint said.

"Coming for you . . . how? To kill you?"

"No, Fitz, that's not what I mean," Clint said. Was Fitz being deliberately dense? "I mean she'll be trying to get me into her bed, like she tries with every man she meets."

"Well, maybe not every man."

"What do you mean?"

"Nothin'," Fitz said. "I just think . . . she hasn't met Art yet, you know?"

"What about your foreman?"

"Don't know if she's met him yet either."

"Okay," Clint said, "let's stop worrying about who the lady's met. I'm just saying she sees me as a challenge, and maybe I can use that."

"What about Bodeen?" Fitz asked. "He's not just going to stand by while you question his wife."

"She's not going to tell him."

"Are you sure?"

"We made a deal."

"What deal?"

"She doesn't tell him, and I owe her."

"So Bodeen's in town talking to the mayor? Is he going to go after that kid detective?"

"Maybe," Clint said. "I hope not. If Fellows gets fired, I'm going to feel responsible."

"So what do we do now?"

"We use your men as watchmen," Clint said. "Six shifts, two men to a shift, two shifts a day for each team. And give them rifles."

"I thought you were going to do that."

"When I agreed to help, Fitz, I said I wasn't a night watchman. I'm going to find out what's going on— me and Fellows. Meanwhile, we'll try to keep your site safe."

"With my men?"

"You want to hire half a dozen guns to do it?" Clint asked.

"I can't justify paying for gunmen, not out of the twenty-five thousand."

"So then we'll use the men you have. Get Steve to pick out the best half-dozen."

"If I know Steve, he'll want to be one of them, so he'll have to pick out five."

"Suits me," Clint said. "I'm going to go back to town with Fellows and see what damage Bodeen has done there. Then I'll come out here and spend the night."

"All right." Fitz took the bottle back, pulled from it, and stopped it up again. "I've got to go back and fight with Art about the plans again. He's constantly trying to change them."

"Why does he keep doing that?"

"Because he's crazy," Fitz said.

"Why did you hire him, then?"

"I didn't. The town hired him before they hired me. I'm stuck with him because he's all I can afford."

"Well, I wish you luck," Clint said. "I'll get Fellows and we'll be on our way."

"Look, Clint," Fitz said, "I wasn't questioning you. I really do appreciate your help."

"That's okay, Fitz."

They walked back to the shack, where Clint retrieved Fellows and Fitz went back to work with Art Sideman.

Clint had decided not to approach Fitz about his own relationship with Cynthia Bodeen. That was best left until later. He doubted very much that Fitz would be sabotaging his own project.

TWENTY-FIVE

Fellows and Clint once again rode back to town. It seemed to Clint there was a lot of riding back and forth going on, without the desired effect.

They didn't pass Patrick Bodeen and his foreman on the way in, so they assumed the men were still in Tucson.

Clint looked over at Fellows, who seemed to be lost in thought.

"You still worried about your job?"

"I have to admit I'm thinking about it," Fellows said. "I came a long way for this position."

"Well, I guess it's my fault you're in danger," Clint said. "Maybe there's something I can do to keep you from being fired."

"Like what?"

"I could talk to the chief, and to the mayor."

"Do you know them?"

"We're certainly not friends," Clint said. "I don't know if they'll listen to me, but I can try."

"Well," Fellows said, "why don't we just wait and see how it turns out? If I do get fired, I certainly won't blame you. I make my own decisions."

"I appreciate that."

Patrick Bodeen sat at a table with Doug Melvin in Hanigan's Saloon, one of the largest in town.

"Boss, are you gonna talk to the chief of police while we're here?" Melvin asked.

"Yeah, I am going to do that," Bodeen said, "but I want you to wait here."

"And do what?"

"Have another drink," Bodeen said. "Just wait for me here."

Melvin shrugged and said, "Sure, Boss."

Bodeen stood up.

"And if you see Adams or that detective, don't talk to them."

"Yessir."

"I'll be right back."

Bodeen left the saloon and walked over to the police station. He was shown immediately into the chief's office.

"I've already spoken with the mayor," Bodeen said to the chief. "Your job is hanging by a thread."

"Maybe throwing you out of here will break that thread," Chief Coleman said, "but I'm still tempted to do it."

"Now look here, it's your detective who's harassing me—"

"He's doing his job," Coleman said. "Up to now you've neither been a help nor a hindrance to the investigation into the vandalism at the university site, and I'm okay with that. But if you do start to hinder the investigation, I won't like it."

Bodeen stared at Coleman in disbelief.

"Are you threatening me?"

"No," Coleman said. "I'm telling you I know you're an influential member of this community, and I respect that. But don't get in the way of me doing my job."

"I got you this job, Robert," Bodeen said. "Do you remember that?"

"Sure I do, Patrick," Coleman said, "but that doesn't put me in your pocket." He patted his girth. "I'm way too big to be in anybody's pocket."

Bodeen stood fuming.

"We'll see about that, Chief," he said. "We'll see."

He stormed out.

Bodeen stormed into the saloon and said to Melvin, "Let's go!"

"But I just got—" Melvin started, looking at his fresh beer.

"We're riding out!" Bodeen snapped.

"Yessir."

They walked outside to their horses, mounted up, and rode out.

As they neared town, Clint and Fellows heard horses galloping toward them. They saw two riders at the same time the riders saw them.

"That's Bodeen and his foreman," Clint said.

"If they draw their guns—"

"They won't," Clint said. "Bodeen won't do that himself. He'd pay someone to do it."

"But if they do—"

Clint looked at Fellows and said, "Then we could end this right here and now."

TWENTY-SIX

As Bodeen and Melvin approached Adams and Fellows, the four of them slowed down, then stopped.

"Been out to my house again?" Bodeen demanded. "Breaking in? Harassing my wife?"

"I think you're wife will tell you there was no harassment, Bodeen," Clint said. "What about you, Bodeen? You get this young man fired just for doing his job?"

"You go to town and find out," Bodeen said.

He urged his horse back into a run and galloped by them with his foreman in tow.

"If she tells him . . ." Fellows said.

"She won't—and you're not fired."

"Why do you say that?"

"If he had managed to get you—or your chief—fired, he would have taken great pleasure in telling us so. And he wouldn't have been so mad. No, he went to town and he didn't get what he wanted."

"I hope you're right."

"Lets go find out."

They rode into town, turned their horses in at the livery, and split up.

"I might as well go right now and find out if you're right," Fellows said.

"I'll see you later, then."

"Where are you going?"

"I think it's time the mayor and I had a talk."

"Good luck."

They went their separate ways.

As soon as Fellows entered the station, the sergeant at the desk said, "The chief's lookin' for you."

"Okay."

He went directly to the chief's office, knocked on the door.

"You wanted to see me?"

Coleman looked up from his desk. Behind him, through the window, Fellows could see horses and wagons going by.

"Come in," the chief said, "and close the door. We have things to discuss, Detective."

Clint walked right to City Hall, wondered if the mayor would see him, or if he'd have to burst in on the man. God, he hated politicians. Even the good ones weren't trustworthy.

He entered the building, found the door that said MAYOR'S OFFICE, and entered. A middle-aged woman seated at a desk looked up at him.

"Can I help you?"

"I'd like to see the mayor."

"Your name?"

"Clint Adams."

She looked at her desk.

"You don't have an appointment."

"No, I don't."

"Sir, you need—"

"Just tell him I'm here."

"Sir—"

"Tell the mayor the Gunsmith is here to see him," Clint said. "Don't make me go in there and announce myself."

She stared at him a moment, then said, "Yes, sir."

"Patrick Bodeen was in here, asking me for your ass," Coleman said.

"Did you give it to him, sir?" the detective asked.

"No, I did not," Coleman said. "Then he threatened my ass."

"Yes, sir?"

"I don't like my ass being threatened, Detective," Coleman said.

"What did you tell him, sir?"

"To get out of my office," Coleman said.

"I mean, about me."

"I told him I don't fire men for doing their jobs," Coleman said.

"Thank you, sir."

"Now do you really think Bodeen is involved in this vandalism?"

"Yes, sir," Fellows said, "I believe it might escalate to assault, and maybe murder, before we're done."

"Well then, Detective," Coleman said, "I suggest you take your still employed ass out there, prove that he's behind it, and stop him before it gets to that point. Understood?"

"Understood, sir."

Fellows got to his feet and left the office.

TWENTY-SEVEN

The woman came out of the mayor's office and said, "You can go in, sir."

"Thank you." He started past her, then stopped and looked at her. "I didn't mean to strong-arm—"

"It doesn't help, sir," she said.

Clint understood, and went into the mayor's office.

As Clint entered, the mayor heaved his bulk out of his chair and stood.

"Mr. Adams," he said. "Have a seat."

"Thank you."

"Can I get you something?"

"Yes," Clint said, "but not the way you mean. Mayor, I need for Detective Fred Fellows not to lose his job. He was only doing—"

"Relax, Mr. Adams," the mayor said, sitting back down. "He's not losing his job."

"And the chief?"

The mayor shook his head.

"Him, neither."

"Well, that's good," Clint said. "And . . . you?"

"I'm going to be in office at least until the next election."

"That's good."

"Bodeen was in here trying to flex his muscles, but he didn't get his way."

"We passed him on the way in," Clint said. "I suspected from his demeanor that he didn't get what he wanted."

"Well now, I'd like to get what I want," the mayor said. "I want to get that university built with no further problems."

"I think we all want that, Mr. Mayor."

"I'm not even sure what your connection to the matter is, Mr. Adams," the mayor said, "but I suggest you go out there and do whatever it is you do to see that it happens."

"Yes, sir," Clint said. "I just wanted to make sure that Mr. Fitzgerald had your complete support."

"We hired him to see that it's built," the mayor said. "That's what I want him to do."

Clint sat there, studying the mayor.

"You're wondering if I'm involved," the politician said. "If, for some reason, I don't want the university built."

"That's what I was thinking."

"And? What's your decision?"

"I think you're clean."

"Why, thank you for that. I'd hate for you to think I'm a liar."

"Well," Clint said, "you are a politician, after all."

The mayor chuckled briefly, then seemed to grow uncomfortable.

"I'll tell Mr. Fitzgerald he still has your blessing," Clint said finally, "and your support."

"Yes," Mayor Darling said, "do that."

Clint nodded, got up, and left.

Steve Taylor came into the shack with the five men he'd chosen to be on watch.

"Fitz, these are—"

"I don't need to be introduced," Fitz said. "Have you given them their shifts?"

"I have." Taylor assumed Fitz didn't need to be introduced to the men because he knew their names. In truth, Fitz had no idea what their names were, and didn't care. He just wanted them on watch.

"Okay, then," Fitz said. "I'll see you all in the morning."

Taylor told the five men to leave. He also turned to leave when Fitz said, "Steve."

"Yeah?"

"Can they handle those rifles?"

"They're the five who can shoot," Steve said. "That's why I picked them."

"I want the next sonofabitch who tries to damage or burn any part of our building shot dead. Is that understood?"

"I understand, Fitz," Taylor said, "but when did you get so bloodthirsty?"

"Just recently, Steve," Fitz said. "And I don't like it."

Taylor nodded, and left the shack.

Sideman, the architect, was asleep in the other room,

snoring rhythmically. Fitz looked at the plans they agreed
would be final. He'd managed to get the man back around
to the original plans.

He walked to the table to roll the plans up and put them
away. As he did, there was a shot, the window broke, and
a bullet went through the plans and into his chest. He
gasped, had only a moment to comprehend what was happening, and then fell dead, facedown on the table.

TWENTY-EIGHT

A knock on his door awoke Clint the next morning. He'd fallen asleep with the Dickens in his hands. It fell to the floor as he got up. He'd only managed to get this boots off, but he'd still made sure his gun was hanging on the bedpost, at the ready. He drew it and took it with him to the door.

When he opened it and saw Fellows, he relaxed and lowered the gun.

"It's pretty early, isn't it?" he asked.

"I have bad news," Fellows said.

"It finally happened?" Clint asked.

Fellows nodded.

"Who was killed?" Clint asked. "How many?"

"One man, Clint."

Clint waited, knew it was bad when Fellows didn't speak right away, then said. "All right, Fred. Who was it?"

"Your friend," Fellows said. "Fitz."

"Damn," Clint said.

* * *

When Clint rode out to the site with Detective Fellows, he was glad to see Chief Coleman there as well.

"I'm sorry about your friend," Coleman said to Clint. "As soon as we learned it was him, I sent Fellows to get you."

"Much obliged," Clint said. "What happened?"

"Near as we can figure," Fellows said, "he was standing at the table, rolling up the set of plans, when a bullet came through the window. Went through the plans and into his chest."

"He was assassinated," Clint said.

"Seems like it," Coleman said.

"Where was Sideman? The architect?"

"Asleep," Fellows said.

"And Taylor, the foreman?"

"On watch," Fellows said, "with another man. They had just set up shifts, two men at a time. The first shift had just started."

"So somebody just sneaked into the camp, shot him, and slipped away."

"Yes," Fellows said.

"Goddamnit!" He looked around. "Where's the body?"

"We sent it to town, to the undertaker's," Coleman said. "Did he have family?"

"No," Clint said. "I'll pay for his burial."

"The town will handle that, I'm sure," Coleman said.

Clint looked around again. Something to hit or shoot at would have been good at that moment.

"We'll find out who did it, Clint," Fellows said.

"I'll find out who did it!" Clint swore.

"Mr. Adams," Coleman said, "I know he was your friend, but—"

"Talk to your mayor," Clint said. "He himself asked me to make sure this building gets built."

"Well, they're going to have to hire somebody to replace Fitzgerald on this project," the chief said.

"I'll take that job."

"You just said you'll be trying to find out who killed Fitz—" Fellows started.

"I'll do both, believe me," Clint said. "I'll catch the killer, the man who hired him, and get this goddamn building built."

"You're sure he was for hire?" Coleman said. "The killer, I mean?"

"Oh, I'm sure," Clint said. "And I'm sure I know who hired it done."

"You're saying Bodeen did it?" Fellows asked.

"I am."

"You're going to have to prove it," Coleman said.

"I will."

He started walking to his horse.

"Sir?" Fellows said to his chief.

"Go on, go with him," Coleman said. "Keep me informed."

Fellows ran to catch up.

Steve Taylor walked over to the chief and asked, "And what do we do?"

"You and your men keep working," Coleman said. "Just keep working."

"Where are you going?" Fellows asked, catching up to Clint.

"There have to be fresh tracks somewhere around here," Clint said. "I'm going to find them."

"I'll come with you."

"Suit yourself," Clint said, "but if I have to run, I'm not going to wait for you."

"Understood."

They mounted up and rode out.

TWENTY-NINE

"What's wrong?" Fellows asked.

Clint stared at the ground, then got up off his knee and looked at Clint.

"They were careful this time," he said. "I think they came a long way on foot."

"Can't you find their boot prints?"

Clint walked back to Eclipse, mounted up, and looked at Fellows.

"If this killer knew what he was doing, he wore moccasins. When he got back to his horse, he might have changed into boots."

"Then how do we find him?"

"We keep looking," Clint said. "There's got to be a likely place for someone to leave their horse for as long as he would have had to, and then walk the rest of the way."

"Yes," Fellows said, "but where?"

"Out there, somewhere," Clint said.

*　*　*

Chief Coleman got back to town and immediately went to the mayor's office.

"What's on your mind, Chief?" Darling asked when the chief was shown in.

"Murder, Mr. Mayor."

"Damn it," Darling said. "It's happened, hasn't it?"

"Yes, sir."

The mayor opened a drawer and took out a bottle of whiskey and a glass. He looked over at the chief, who nodded, and then took out a second glass. He poured them both half full and passed one to the chief. It was not yet 10 a.m.

"Who was killed?" the mayor asked.

"Fitzgerald."

"How?"

"Murdered," Coleman said. "Shot."

"Damn it, again. Do we know who did it?"

"The Gunsmith thinks he knows."

"Is he going after Bodeen?"

"He thinks Bodeen hired it done," Coleman said. "First he'll find the man that did it, then the man who hired him."

Darling sat back, finished his drink, then leaned forward and poured another. He offered it to the chief, who waved it away. He had not yet finished his first.

"We'll have to hire somebody to replace Fitzgerald," the mayor said.

"Adams wants that job."

"He's out manhunting."

"He still says he'll get the university built."

"What do you think?"

"I believe him."

"I'll have to get the council's okay."

"You're the mayor," Coleman said. "Do what you have to do."

"We haven't always seen eye to eye, Robert," Darling said. "Will you back me on this? The Gunsmith to replace Fitzgerald?"

"I will."

"All right, then," the mayor said. "I'll call a meeting this afternoon."

"I'll be there," Coleman said. He finished his drink and set the glass on the desk. Standing up, he said again, "I'll be there," and left.

THIRTY

Clint and Fellows rode in circles for most of the day. At no time were they more than a couple of hours from the university site.

"It'll be dark soon," Fellows said. "We have no provisions to stay out all night."

"We'll go back to the site, eat, stay there, and head out in the morning," Clint said, "with some provisions. Tomorrow I'm going to find this sonofabitch's trail."

"We still have a little daylight," Fellows said.

"I've got to go back, talk to the foreman and the architect, and to the men," Clint said. "We'll need to put out more than two men at a time on watch."

"Do you think they'll accept you as their new boss?" the detective asked.

"Let's ride back and find out."

They got back to the site just as it was getting dark. They saw the campfires from a distance, smelled the food cooking as they got closer.

Steve Taylor greeted them as they rode in.

"Anything?" he asked.

"Not yet," Clint said, dismounting.

"Are you taking over?" Taylor asked.

"Is that what you heard from town?" Clint asked.

"We haven't heard a thing," Taylor said. "It just makes sense to me."

"What about your men? Will it make sense to them?" Clint asked.

"It will if I tell them it will," Taylor said. "You tell me what you want them to do, and I'll see to it they do it."

"And what about Sideman?"

"Can I speak frankly?"

"Of course."

"We don't need an architect anymore," Taylor said. "All he is now is a lot of trouble, always trying to change the plans. I say ship him back where he came from."

"He's not needed if there's a problem?"

"The only problems we're having are coming from without, Clint," Taylor said. "We don't need him to come up with problems from within. I say pay him off."

"I understand."

"There's stew tonight."

"Thanks."

Clint and Fellows went and ate with the men. After eating, Clint explained to the men about the increased watches.

"Didn't help last night, did it?" one man said. "Mr. Fitzgerald ended up dead."

"That's why we're going to increase the watch," Clint said. "Four men at a time, with rifles."

"We're builders," another man said, "not gunmen."

"Don't worry," Clint said. "There will be three shifts. I'll be on one, Detective Fellows on a second, and Steve Taylor on the third."

"And what are we guarding?" another man asked. "Are we gonna continue with the building?"

"Definitely," Clint said. "I'll be taking Mr. Fitzgerald's place."

"What do you know about—"

"I know about getting a job done," Clint said. "As for the actual building knowledge, I'll depend on you and Mr. Taylor for that. I'm not going to try to tell you what to do, I'm just going to make sure it gets done."

"And Mr. Taylor stays foreman?"

"Yes."

"And Mr. Sideman?" another man asked. "Do we have to put up with him?"

"No," Clint said, "I think Mr. Sideman's work here is done."

The men cheered and one asked, "Who's going to tell him, sir?"

"I'll be doing that," Clint said, "probably in the morning. Mr. Taylor will now give you your shifts. He will either choose the men who'll stand watch, or you can volunteer."

Clint went and sat down next to Fellows, who was having coffee. He poured a cup for Clint and handed it to him.

"Looks like they're volunteering," Fellows said.

"That's good," Clint said. "Volunteers work harder than draftees."

"Are we still going back out tomorrow?"

"Yes," Clint said. "I wouldn't be doing anyone any

good here. Taylor can handle the men." He looked at the detective. "Do you want to go back to town?"

"No," Fellows said. "There's no need. My case is out here."

"No lady in town?"

"No."

"Your boss won't mind?"

"He'd probably prefer it."

"All right, then," Clint said. "You can bunk in with the men."

"Is there room?"

"That's what we'll find out."

"What about you?"

"I'll be bunking in with the architect."

"Before or after you fire him?" Fellows asked.

"That's a good point," Clint said.

"If you fire him first, and then you're killed during the night, I'll have to suspect him and arrest him."

"Okay," Clint said, "you're right. I won't fire him until the morning."

"And you don't have to say 'fired,'" Fellows suggested. "Why don't you find another word?"

"Like what?"

"Hmm . . . you're not much firing him as his job is done, finished. He's not needed anymore."

"So I should just . . . let him go," Clint said. "Tell him his services are no longer needed."

"Exactly."

"I'll try that," Clint said. "We'll see how that works out."

"What could he do?" Fellows asked. "He's just an architect."

THIRTY-ONE

Clint didn't have time to deal with—or even interact with—Art Sideman that night. When he went into the shack to sleep, the architect was snoring away. The shack smelled sour, obviously a result of the man's body odor and hygiene. Clint went to sleep, determined to deal with him in the morning.

The smell of coffee woke him up early. He went outside and found a couple of fires with bacon sizzling and coffee brewing over them. He was eating bacon and drinking coffee when Art Sideman came stumbling out of the shack, no pants on, just long underwear. He grabbed a cup of coffee without speaking to anyone, and Clint could see why the men didn't want him around anymore.

Fellows ambled over, sat next to Clint, and started to eat.

"Gonna take care of the architect today?"

"As soon as I finish eating," Clint said. "I think it'll

do wonders for the men's morale not to have him stumbling around here in his long johns."

Fellows looked over at the architect, who was still staggering around, at times scratching his butt through his underwear, and said, "I agree."

Clint finished his breakfast. By that time, Sideman was back inside the shack. When Clint entered, he saw the man once again bent over a set of plans. These plans had a hole through them, and some bloodstains on them, but were still readable.

"Mr. Sideman," Clint said.

"Huh?" Sideman looked up at Clint. His face was sweaty and heavily stubbled, his eyes red-rimmed.

"Clint Adams, remember?"

Sideman stared at him for a few moments, then said, "Oh, yes, of course, Mr. Fitzgerald's friend."

"Well, I was Mr. Fitzgerald's friend," Clint said, "but he's dead."

"Yes, of course I know that!" Sideman snapped. "I'm not a child."

"Good. If you're not a child, then you'll understand that your job is done here."

"What?"

"It's time for you to go, Art."

The man stood up straight and ignored the plans for a change.

"What are you trying to tell me?"

"I'm not trying to tell you," Clint said, "I am telling you that you're done here. Time to go."

"You are presuming to fire me?"

"I'm not presuming anything," Clint said. "And I'm

not firing you. It's just that you're finished. You've been paid, and you're done."

"These plans—"

"The plans are fine," Clint said. "You can't keep changing them. It's done. We want you to go."

"Who wants me to go?"

"Everyone."

"Does Mr. Taylor know about this? He is, after all, the foreman."

"He's the foreman, but I'm in charge now," Clint said. "However, if you need to hear it from him, I'll send him in."

"Please do! And what about Mr. Eiland?"

"I haven't met Mr. Eiland. Does he ever come out here?"

"Mr. Eiland stays at the best hotel in town," Sideman said. "He represents the university."

"Well, you go and tell Mr. Eiland what's going on," Clint said, "and if he wants to talk to me, he can come out here. I have the blessing of the town council and the mayor." He was lying, but he thought it would be true eventually. "After you talk to Steve, I'd like you to pack up and leave."

And when the man was gone, Clint was going to open all the doors and windows and air the shack out.

He left and went in search of Steve Taylor.

"So he's fired?" Taylor asked.

"He's not fired, he's done, finished, his job is over," Clint said. "Just tell him to go."

"Okay," Taylor said happily. "No problem. I'll do it."

"Good."

"What are you going to be doing?"

"Fellows and I are going to go out again to look for tracks. There's got to be something somewhere."

"Fine," Taylor said. "I'll get rid of Sideman and keep the men working."

"Very good. We'll most likely see you later tonight, but I'm going to take some provisions in case we have to camp out."

"Okay, that's fine."

"Oh, one more thing," Clint said. "After he leaves, air that shack out."

"Gotcha," Taylor said with a smile.

Clint watched Taylor go to finish the dirty work, then turned and looked for Fellows. The man was still eating, and raised his coffee cup to Clint.

"Finish that plate and let's go," he said to the detective.

"What? I was gonna have more. I haven't had food like this before. It really tastes better when you eat it out here, from a campfire."

"Well, we're going to take some stuff with us in case we have to stay out overnight."

"You mean camp and sleep on the trail?"

"That's what I mean."

The young man stood up excitedly.

"I've never done that," he said. "Can I build the fire?"

"I don't know," Clint said. "Can you? I guess we're going to find out."

THIRTY-TWO

Clint and Fellows spent the rest of the morning and the afternoon looking for a trail left by a killer. By late afternoon Clint was becoming frustrated.

"This isn't right," he said to Fellows. "There has to be a trail. There can't have been a horse or a wagon out here without leaving a trail."

"What if there wasn't one?"

"What?"

"No, horse," Fellows said, "and no wagon."

"You mean . . . the killer walked all the way? Maybe from the Bodeen ranch? You know how many miles that is?"

"No," Fellows said, "but it doesn't matter, because that's not what I'm talking about."

"Then what are you talking about?"

"I'm talking about someone from within," Fellows said.

"Somebody who was already in the camp."

"You mean, the vandalism, the fires, and now the murder were committed by someone already in the camp? Working in the camp?"

"That's what I'm saying."

Clint stared at the detective.

"You don't think so?"

"I think that's brilliant," Clint said, looking around them. "That's why there are no tracks."

"Well, it's a theory."

"No, no," Clint said, "that's it. That's the answer."

"Then we have to go back and question everyone in the camp," Fellows said. "Tracking is what you do, but investigating is what I do."

"Okay," Clint said. "When we get back to camp, you take the lead, and I'll follow."

They headed back to camp.

"Can we eliminate Steve Taylor?" Clint asked.

"Why?"

"Well, he's the foreman," Clint said. "Why would he want to sabotage the project?"

"I don't know," Fellows said, "but I think it's way too soon to eliminate anyone."

"Well, except you and me."

"Especially since we weren't even in camp when it happened," the detective pointed out.

"Good point."

"All right," Clint said. "Let's go back to camp and find out who the murdering spy is."

While Clint and Fellows were out looking for tracks, Art Sideman packed his things and left the site, riding into town. He rode directly to the Silver Spur Hotel and went up to George Eiland's suite. He banged on the door until the man answered.

"What the hell are you doing here?" Eiland demanded.

"I got kicked out."

"What?"

"Off the site."

"By who?"

"Clint Adams."

"Clint—what the hell does he have to do with anything?"

"You haven't been keeping up, Eiland," Sideman said. "Now that Fitzgerald is dead, Adams is taking over."

"The Gunsmith?" Eiland said. "Now we have to deal with him?"

"Well," Art Sideman said, "you should have thought of that before you had me kill Fitzgerald."

THIRTY-THREE

When Clint and Fellows returned to the site, Art Side-man was gone.

"He left as soon as I told him you were in charge," Taylor told Clint as he dismounted. "Did you find the trail you were lookin' for?"

"Yeah, we did," Clint said. "It led us right back here."

"What?"

"Come with me," Clint said. He took Taylor into the shack and closed the door. He explained Fellow's theory to the foreman.

"I'm taking you into my confidence, Steve," Clint said, "because I don't believe you're the guy."

"Well, I apprec—"

"But if I find out you are the guy, I'll make you the sorriest sonofabitch who ever lived. You got that?"

"I've got it, Clint," Taylor said. "Believe me, it wasn't me."

"Okay, then," Clint said, "you, me, and the detective are going to find out who it was."

"How?"

"By questioning the men one by one," Clint said.

"Are we gonna hold up work for that?" Taylor asked.

"No, keep the men working," Clint said. "Fellows and I will set up in here, then you send them in one by one. Fellows will question them. That's what he does. He'll figure out who it is."

"The men are gonna talk among themselves when they come out."

"We'll tell them not to," Clint said. "A few of them still might, and if the word gets to the guilty man, maybe he'll run for it. Then we'll know who it is."

"Okay," Taylor said, "I get it."

"Good," Clint said, "then let's get started. Give Fellows some time to get set up in here."

"How will I know how much time?"

"Ask him, then send him in here," Clint said. "With any luck, we can get this resolved today, and then go back to building this university without any worries."

Taylor walked to the door, then stopped.

"What's wrong?"

"I don't like the idea that a killer's been working among my men, and I didn't know about it."

"If I'm right," Clint said, "then he's a professional. It's his job to fool you. Don't feel bad, Steve. Just help us catch the sonofabitch."

"You got it, Clint."

Fellows came in and Clint watched while he set up the table and some chairs the way he wanted them.

"Where do you want me?" Clint asked.

"I want you to stand behind them while they're seated.

I want them to be wondering what you're doing back there at all times."

"Okay."

"And if it's all right with you, I want to introduce you to them again. I want to make sure they know you're the Gunsmith. We can use that against them."

"Suits me," Clint said. "Whatever you want to do. I'm going to watch you work."

"Okay," Fellows said. "Let Taylor know he can start sending them in."

"Will do."

"I just hope I'm as good at this as I think I am," the detective said.

THIRTY-FOUR

"Well," Clint said, "you were right."

"About what?" Fellows asked.

"You are good at this."

It was late, they had seen all the men, given them about ten minutes each, and now it was time to have something to eat.

"But . . . it's none of them," Fellows said.

"What?"

"From what I can see," Fellows said, "the killer is not among them."

"That doesn't mean you weren't good at it," Clint said. "You had them all . . . mesmerized."

"Well, it helped that the Gunsmith was standing behind them. They were scared stiff."

"And now that they know we suspected them all," Clint remarked, "we have to go out there and eat with them."

"I don't think that's going to be a problem," Fellows

said. "They all liked Fitz. They want to help find his killer."

"What about Taylor?" Clint asked. "Am I wrong about him?"

"No," Fellows said. "It's not him."

"Who then?" Clint asked. "Who's left? We talked to everybody."

They looked at each other.

"I'm hungry," Fellows said. "Let's get something to eat. In the morning, I'll have to go back to town and talk to the chief."

"Yeah, okay," Clint said. "I'll ride back with you."

They left the shack, walked to one of the fires, where they each got a plate of beans and a cup of coffee.

"Take some biscuits," Reacher, the man cooking, said. "They're hard, but dip 'em in the beans."

"Okay, thanks," Clint said.

"That architect, he liked my biscuits," Reacher said. "Now that he's gone, somebody has to eat them."

They each took two biscuits, then carried their meager meals to the shack.

"Wait a minute," Clint said in the middle of their meal.

"What?"

"We haven't talked to everybody."

"What do you mean?"

"Sideman."

"The architect!" Fellows said. "We haven't talked to him."

"We let him go!" Clint said.

"Chased him back to town," Fellows said. "But . . . the architect?"

"What better way to avoid suspicion?" Clint said.

"You don't think he was a real architect?" Fellows asked.

Clint shrugged. "I don't know. What if that's the reason he was always trying to change the plans?"

"Let's talk to Steve," Fellows said. "He may have some insight."

"And tomorrow we can ride into town and question Sideman," Clint said.

"If that's his real name."

"Isn't there someone else?" Clint asked. "Someone who represents the university?"

"George Eiland," Fellows said. "He sits in on town council meetings. He's friends with the mayor."

"That sounds like somebody we should talk to also," Clint said.

THIRTY-FIVE

By morning Clint was convinced they'd made a terrible error letting Art Sideman go. The more he thought about it, the more sense it made that Sideman—or whoever he was—was the saboteur, and the killer. They just needed to find him to make sure.

He came out of the shack and started to saddle Eclipse. Fellows came along and saddled his horse.

Taylor told them that he'd never met "Art Sideman" before he came to the site, and that was the same time Fitz had met him. The architect and Fitz had corresponded with each other, and Fitz had received the original plans in the mail. It was only when Sideman came to the site that all the other versions of the plans started to appear.

"The funny thing," Taylor said, "is that they didn't look like they'd been drawn up by the same man."

That was enough to convince Clint that "Art Sideman" was a fake.

"You ready to go?" he asked Fellows.

"I'm ready."

They mounted up.

When they reached town, they turned their horses in at the livery.

"I've got to go and see the chief, tell him what's going on," Fellows said.

"Why don't I come along?" Clint said.

"Sure, why not? Maybe it won't sound so crazy coming from both of us."

"It's not crazy at all," Clint said. "Someone hired the man to impersonate the architect, sabotage the project, maybe even damage it enough to halt the construction. Finally, he decided to commit murder."

"And then we kicked him out of camp."

"Well," Clint said, "that may sound crazy. Look, I'll take the blame for that."

"No, you won't," Fellows said. "I told you, I make my own decisions."

"Okay, but I'll back you up."

"I'd appreciate it."

They walked from the livery stable to the police station, and as they entered, the young sergeant at the desk gave Clint a dirty look and said to Fellows, "Chief's looking for you."

THIRTY-SIX

"Are you sure about this?" the chief asked.

Fellows and Clint exchanged a look.

"We're fairly sure, sir," Fellows said.

"And you let him go?"

"We weren't sure at that time, Chief," Clint said.

"And where did he go?"

"We're assuming he came here," Fellows said.

"And if he's left town?"

"We'll have to find him," Clint said.

"Okay, look," Chief Coleman said, "find out where Fitzgerald found this architect, and send a telegram. Maybe the real one is still there."

"We can check with that other man . . . what did you say his name was?" Clint asked.

"Who's he talking about?" Coleman said.

"George Eiland," Fellows said, answering both of them. "He represents the university people. He'll know where the architect came from."

"Fine," Coleman said, "talk to him, but take care. He's friends with the mayor."

"Yessir."

They got up to leave and the chief said, "Hang back a minute, Fellows."

"Yessir. See you out front, Clint."

Clint nodded and left. Fellows turned to face the chief. "Sir?"

"I just want you to be careful."

"About what, sir?"

"Adams."

"What about him?"

"Just watch how much trouble he gets you into."

"Sir, I can think for myself."

"I know you can, son. Like I said, I'm just warning you."

"Yessir. I'll keep that in mind."

"That's all."

Fellows nodded, left the office, and went outside, where he found Clint waiting for him on the street.

"What was that about?"

"He just wanted to warn me."

"About Eiland?"

"About you."

"Me?"

"He seems to think you're going to get me into trouble."

"Now what are the chances?" Clint asked.

They walked over to the Silver Spur Hotel, got George Eiland's room number from the clerk, and then went up to the third floor to knock on the door of the man's suite.

"Fancy place," Clint said, "although you've probably seen the like or better in the East."

"I'm sure you've seen better in your travels."

"Okay," Clint nodded, "let's agree it's nice, but we've both seen better."

The door opened and Eiland appeared. Clint was not surprised to see a man in his fifties, wearing a three-piece suit and looking like he'd be at home in a university.

"Mr. Eiland?" Fellows asked.

"Yes?"

"My name is Detective Fellows, from the Tucson Police," Fellows said. "This is my colleague, Clint Adams."

"Colleague?" Eiland said. "I was unaware that the Gunsmith had joined the Tucson Police Department."

"Unofficially," Clint said. "I'm sort of . . . an advisor."

"I see."

"May we come in, Mr. Eiland?" Fellows asked. "We have some questions."

"Of course. Come in." Eiland backed away to allow them to enter. They found themselves in one room of a large two-room suite. "Is this about the trouble out at the site?"

"It is," Fellows asked. "We'd like to know where your architect came from."

"I'm sorry. . . where he came from?"

"Where he lived when you found him," Clint said.

"Why don't you ask him?" Eiland asked. For Clint's money the look on his face was way too innocent to be genuine.

"I'm afraid he's gone missing," Clint said. "You haven't seen him in the past couple of days, have you?"

"I'm afraid not."

"We're wondering if he returned home," Fellows said. "We figure we'll send a telegram to his home and see if he responds."

"Hmm, well, I have to tell you, I'm not sure," Eiland said. "Ted Fitzgerald handled all of that."

"No idea?" Clint asked. "I mean, you were paying the man. You must have some idea where he was from."

"Well, back East, of course, but exactly where . . . I'm afraid I'm at a loss. Wouldn't Ted have had that written down somewhere?"

"I'm sure he did," Clint said. He looked at Fellows. "We'll have to go back to the site and check."

"Well then, we better get started," Fellows said. "Thank you, Mr. Eiland."

"Thank you, gentlemen, for all the work you're doing to help get this university finished."

Both men nodded, and left.

"I don't have to be a detective to know he was lying," Clint said down in the lobby.

"Oh yes," Fellows said. "He knows more than he's saying."

"If he knows the phony Sideman, he's going to have to tell him that we're going to the site to check on the real architect's home. They're not going to want us to be able to contact him. Not yet anyway."

"So you think Sideman will go back to the site to try and get that information before we do?"

"I don't see how he could figure that," Clint said. "For all Eiland knows, we're already on our way out there. No way he can beat us there."

"Well then," Fellows said, "maybe he'll try to stop us on the way back."

"Good point," Clint said.

Once again they went to saddle up for a ride out to the site.

THIRTY-SEVEN

George Eiland waited long enough for Clint Adams and Detective Fellows to go down to the lobby, then left his room and hurried down the hall to another door. He pounded on it frantically until it was open. The man standing in the door had little resemblance to "Art Sideman" but it was the same man.

"What the hell—"

"You've got to get back to the site."

"What for?"

"Adams and that detective are on their way back there."

"Come inside before somebody sees you," the man said calmly.

As Eiland entered, the other man closed the door.

"Now calm down and tell me what's going on," the man instructed.

Eiland told the man about his visit from Clint and Fellows.

"So they're going back there to search Fitzgerald's records," the man said. "Well, yeah, they'll find out, all right."

"You've got to stop them!" Eiland said. "We don't want them sending a telegram to the real Sideman."

"I should have killed him when we decided to impersonate him," the man said.

"Well, don't just stand there. Get going!"

"Relax," the phony Sideman said. "There's no way I can beat them there."

"Then what will you do?"

"I'll just have to catch them on the way back."

Steve Taylor was surprised to see Clint and Fellows ride into camp.

"You fellas back already?" he asked. "You sure must like that ride back and forth."

"I'm starting to really hate it," Clint said. "But we need to find some information in the shack."

"What information?"

"We need to know where Art Sideman lived before he came to work here," Fellows said.

"We figure Fitz had it written down somewhere."

"You don't need to look for it," Taylor said. "Sideman came from a town in North Carolina called Golina."

"Are you sure?" Clint asked.

"Positive."

"You didn't get that information from Sideman himself, did you?" Fellows asked.

"No," Taylor said, "Fitz told me about it."

Fellows looked at Clint, who said, "Good enough for me."

"But we don't want to head back too soon," the detective said.

"No," Clint said. "Coffee?"

"Why not?"

Taylor looked at both men like they were nuts.

Clint and Fellows each had a leisurely cup of coffee and watched the men work while they drank it.

"Okay," Clint said. "That should do it."

"So, you're actually giving this guy time to get set up to ambush you?" Taylor asked.

"We need him to do it in order to give himself up," Clint said.

"Yeah, but what if he kills you?" Taylor asked. "Or one of you?"

"We'll just have to see to it that he doesn't," Clint said.

The man who was "Art Sideman" rode out of Tucson at a leisurely pace, intending to find a likely place for an ambush.

Much of his work was done from ambush. On occasion, he did more close-up work, like the killing of Ted Fitzgerald. Most of his close-up work was simply setup, like establishing himself as "Art Sideman" before beginning his work as a saboteur. But his killing he preferred to do at a distance. Not because he didn't like the sight or smell of blood. In truth, he did. Blood was usually an indication that he had done his job correctly. He simply preferred using a rifle to using a handgun. He was not a gunman; he was a killer. There was a big difference. Clint Adams was a gunman, and it would be foolish for the man to face him on even terms with a handgun. No, the way to kill the Gunsmith was from a distance. It was a job, and he didn't particularly care if he became known for killing him or not.

As long as he got paid.

THIRTY-EIGHT

Clint and Fellows headed back to Tucson at a leisurely pace.

"Are you sure about this?" Fellows asked.

"Look," Clint said, "putting a man in a room and questioning him is what you do. This is what I do. There are several places which would be good for an ambush. I'm going to be the target, while you watch my back."

"How do you know I can watch your back?" Fellows asked. "You've never even seen me shoot."

"Well, we don't have time for me to test you," Clint said. "I'll just have to take your word for it that you *can* shoot."

"I never said I could shoot," Fellows pointed out.

Clint gave him a look.

"I'm just kidding," the detective said.

"Wrong time, wrong place," Clint said.

"Okay, sorry," Fellows said. "So I can shoot . . . a little."

*   *   *

The killer got himself into position, comfortable with the rifle in his hands. He was lying on his belly on top of a smooth boulder, with a clear view of the road below. Since it was a straight run on the road from Tucson to the site and back, he expected Adams and the detective to use the road. If they didn't, then he was going to have to figure something else out.

He took off his hat and made himself comfortable.

"Okay," Clint said, reining in. "Here's where we split up."

"Are you sure about this?"

"Dead sure."

"What about when he sees you alone?" Fellows asked. "Isn't he going to wonder where I am?"

"I'm hoping he'll think you stayed at the site while I'm riding back."

"What if he's a really good shot and he kills you?" Fellows asked.

"Then you better get him," Clint said. "You circle around, look for the cluster of rocks I told you about."

"I'll do it," Fellows said, "but I don't feel good about it."

"Go," Clint said. "We both let this guy go. Let's make up for that."

"Agreed."

Fellows rode his horse in a semicircle. He knew where Clint had told him the rocks were, but he spent more time in the city than on horseback. He was afraid he was going to get lost, and get Clint killed.

Just follow the directions, he told himself.

* * *

Clint gave Fellows a little time to get himself into position, then started forward. He stuck to the road, to make it easy for the killer to find him. He just hoped that the absence of Fellows wouldn't tip the killer off that he was in a trap. If the man sensed the danger and rode off, they might never get another chance to catch him. Then having let him go—and not just let him go but actually kicking him out of camp—would stick with them for a very long time.

In the past, Clint had been very good about sensing ambush. It was a sixth sense that had helped him to live this long. In addition, Eclipse had saved his life more than once by warning him. Now he was going to have to depend on both their senses to survive this moment.

He thought he knew where the man, the false Sideman, would shoot from. If he was wrong, it might cost him dearly.

"Ears up, boy," he said, patting Eclipse's neck, "nostrils open."

Eclipse lifted his head up, as if he was sniffing the air.

"That's it, big boy," Clint said. "Maybe between the both of us, we can keep me alive."

The false Art Sideman heard a rider approaching at a trot, perked up, and shouldered his rifle. It bothered him that he heard only one rider. There could have been a couple of explanations for that. Either one of them had stayed behind, or they were trying to trap him.

The killer's talent had taken him this far in his chosen profession, and had kept him alive. But mixed in with that talent was a necessary degree of arrogance. In the execution of his various jobs he'd had to balance the two perfectly.

And this was no different.

However, the fact that when the lone rider came into sight, it was the Gunsmith, and not the policeman, pushed him over the edge into arrogance. How could he give up this chance of killing the Gunsmith? Even if he didn't care who knew he'd done it, he'd know—and he'd always know if he walked away from the chance.

Wherever the policeman was, he was no match for the killer.

He lifted the rifle and sighted down the barrel.

Fellows was worried that his worst fear had come true, and he was lost—and then he came within sight of the rock formation that Clint had told him about.

"A killer could take cover behind it," Clint had told him, "but what I would do is climb up on top of it for the best view I could get, and the best angle."

And there he was!

THIRTY-NINE

Fellows saw the man with the rifle on top of the rocks. He also saw, in the distance, Clint come riding into view. Now he had to do something to make sure that Clint didn't end up dead.

He kicked his horse in the ribs, urging him into a run. He drew his handgun, knowing he was too far away for it to be of any use, but all he really wanted to do was make some noise.

He pulled the trigger.

The killer heard the first shot, and it caused him to rush his own. He pulled the trigger a split second before he should have, and cursed.

Clint heard the first shot, knew from the sound that it was a handgun, not a rifle.

It was Fellows.

He launched himself from the saddle just as he heard the crack of a rifle.

Fellows continued to pull the trigger of his gun until it was empty, then he holstered it and urged his horse on faster. As he neared the rocks, saw the shooter stand up, he drew his own rifle out, but he was not good with a rifle, and had certainly never made a shot from the saddle.

In trying to save Clint's life, he never meant to give up his own, but that might be the way it ended up.

The man on the rocks turned his attention toward him.

Clint drew his rifle as he leaped from his saddle. When he hit the ground, he gave up his hip in order to keep his hold on the rifle. Without his hands to break his fall, he took the brunt of it on the left hip. He had to ignore the pain, though. He rolled and came up in a crouch, facing the shooter on the rock. He could see that the shooter had switched targets, and was now facing Fellows, who was a sitting duck.

The killer knew he had to move fast. Fire at one approaching horseman, and then at the other, who was now on the ground. He knew the Gunsmith had hit the ground hard. He only hoped it would take the man several seconds to collect himself.

He aimed his rifle at Fellows.

The detective saw the man pointing his weapon at him. He reined his horse in and had to make a decision. Aim and fire, or hit the ground?

Feeling he had given Clint the time he needed, he decided to hit the ground.

*   *   *

Clint knew he had to act or Fellows was dead—and the young detective had pretty much saved his life. He had known the shooter would be on that rock, and yet the man might have gotten his shot off in time.

Now it was his turn.

He shouldered his rifle, and fired.

FORTY

Fellows hit the ground and rolled, but not having the instincts or reflexes of Clint Adams, he ended up on his back. He was vulnerable, but had probably landed—by pure luck—in the position that afforded the killer his smallest target.

In addition, his rifle had flown from his hand on impact, so he stayed where he was, waiting for the shot and hoping for the best.

The killer swore.

The policeman was flat on his back, presenting a difficult target, especially since the ground was not completely flat.

Angry at himself, knowing he had let his arrogance get the best of him, he turned to find Clint Adams in his sights—but instead, turned right into the Gunsmith's bullet.

* * *

Clint saw the man prepare to fire, then apparently change his mind. He then turned toward Clint, who had already pulled the trigger.

The bullet hit the man squarely and threw him off the rock.

As the killer flew through the air, he started to curse himself, but he was cut short when he hit the ground. The air went out of his lungs, but before he could try to breathe in again, he was dead.

Fellows got up off the ground, looked around. He walked over and picked up his rifle, then walked toward his horse, which was standing calmly a few feet away. He mounted up and rode toward the rocks.

Clint looked around, saw Eclipse standing a few yards away. He started to walk toward him, but his hip screamed and he stopped. Instead, he whistled and the Darley Arabian came trotting over. Clint struggled into the saddle and rode for the rocks.

Fellows and Clint reached the body at the same time.

"Check him," Clint said. "See if he's alive."

He couldn't dismount, so Fellows did it, walked to the body, and leaned over it.

"He's dead."

"Disarm him."

"I said he's dead."

"Disarm him anyway."

Fellows leaned over, took the man's gun from his holster, and stuck it in his belt.

He walked back to Clint and looked up at him. "You okay?"

"I landed on my hip. You?"

"Broke my fall with my hands." He held out his scraped palms.

"I held on to my rifle," Clint said.

"Lucky for both of us."

"Luck had nothing to do with it. I needed the rifle."

"And not your hip?"

"It'll heal."

"We better get you back to town so the doctor can have a look," Fellows said.

"You, too," Clint said.

"We'll send somebody back for the body."

"His horse has to be around here someplace," Clint said. "Let's find it. We can tie the body to it and take it in ourselves."

Fellows grinned. "That means I'm going to have to tie it to the saddle, right?"

"I'll go and find it," Clint said. "I can do that from the saddle."

"Fine."

"Find his rifle, too," Clint said.

Fellows nodded.

Fellows tied a tight knot so the body wouldn't slide off during the ride back.

"Okay," he said. "That does it." He mounted his own

horse, looked at Clint, whose face was pale and etched with pain. "You okay?"

"I will be. Let's get back to town. I'm starting to think you're right."

"About what?"

"I think I need a doctor."

FORTY-ONE

"That's gonna be black-and-blue tomorrow," the doctor told Clint.

Clint was lying on the doctor's table, naked and in pain.

"Nothing's broke, Doc?" he asked. "It feels like something's broken."

"No, just bruised," the doctor said. "You'll be all right. Oh, it's gonna hurt for a while. Take this over to the apothecary and they'll give you something for the pain."

Clint stood up, took the piece of paper the doctor offered.

"Get dressed. I'll see you outside."

Clint and Fellows had ridden in, brought the body to the undertaker's, and then Fellows helped him to the doctor. From there the detective went to tell his chief what happened. They agreed to meet at the hotel later.

Clint got dressed and limped out of the examining room into the doctor's front office.

"What do I owe you, Doc?"

"Two dollars should do it," the doctor said. His name was Brady. He was in his forties, had set up practice in Tucson just five years before.

"If you have any problems, come back and see me, Mr. Adams," the doctor said. "But you should heal up okay."

"Thanks, Doc."

Clint left the doctor's office and limped over to the apothecary. He went in and handed the paper he'd gotten from the doctor over to the clerk.

"I'll be right with you, sir."

While he waited, the door opened and a woman walked in.

"Well, Mr. Adams."

He looked at her face and recognized her,

"Cynthia," he said. "You look lovely."

"You look like a mess," she said. "I hear you got the man who killed your friend."

"Has the word gotten out already?"

"Oh, yeah," she said. "The word's gotten around. But is that going to stop what's been going on?"

"Probably not," Clint said. "I've still got to find the man he was working for. Is that your husband, Cynthia?"

"My husband? He's not smart enough to be behind this."

"You don't think so?"

"No."

The clerk came back, gave Clint the powder the doctor had prescribed for his pain. He limped to the door.

"Why don't I help you over to your hotel, Clint?" she asked. "We can discuss things further there."

"Sure," Clint said, "Sure, I could use help walking back to my hotel."

"Good," she said. "Let's go."

She helped him walk to the Palace, then he really had to lean on her to get up the stairs. By the time they got to his room, his hip was throbbing.

She deposited him on the bed, then took the powder from him and mixed it in water for him.

"Here, this will help with the pain. I know, I've used it myself."

"It won't put me to sleep, will it?"

"No. It'll just help with the pain."

He drank it.

"If you're worried, I can stay with you while you get some sleep," she said. "I'll make sure nobody comes in to kill you."

"There won't be anyone to do that, not yet," Clint said. "Not until they replace the man Fellows and I brought in."

"Do you know his name?"

"Not yet, but we'll find out."

"Let me help you with your boots."

She slipped both of his boots off as gently as she could, dropped them to the floor.

"You know, it wasn't a coincidence we met today," she said. "I saw you go into the apothecary."

"That's good," he said. "I don't believe in co-incidence."

She put her hand on his left leg.

"Is this the hip?"

"It is."

"Come on, let me take off your pants. Maybe it'll feel better if I rub it."

He didn't fight her. He let her take off his gun belt, told her to hang it on the bedpost. Then she slipped off his trousers.

She moved to the other side of the bed, sat down, and began to rub her hands over his thigh and hip. She was right, it did feel better. Or maybe it was the powder. Either way, her touch felt good.

Real good.

FORTY-TWO

She rubbed his hip, his thigh, then his belly. Slowly she moved her hand down until she slid it into his shorts. She closed her hand over his penis and it began to swell.

"This part of you seems all right," she said.

"I didn't fall on that part," he said.

She slid his underwear down and off, then put her hands on his legs, rubbed both thighs, then gently spread them apart.

"That hurt?"

"Not so bad."

"If I hurt you, you let me know."

"I'll scream."

She dug her nails unto his thighs, smiled wickedly, and said, "That won't necessarily mean you're hurting."

She took his cock in both hands, stroked it lovingly until it was long and hard and throbbing, and then took it into her mouth.

She began to suck on him, wetting him thoroughly, moaning as she rode him up and down with her mouth.

He groaned, and she released him from the velvet grip of her mouth.

"I hurt you?"

"It hurts so good," he said.

She smiled, stood up, and started to undress. He'd wondered how she would took naked. Now he knew. She was tall, long-legged, and heavy-breasted. Her skin was pale and smooth, and her flesh seemed to glow in the light from the window.

She got in bed with him, both of them naked.

"I'm not going to be able to move much," he warned her.

"Don't worry," she said. "I'll do all the moving for both of us."

She kissed him, on the mouth, the neck, the stomach. She worked her way back down to his still hard penis and went to work on it again, with her hands and her mouth. She got him to the point where he had to grit his teeth to keep from shouting, but it still wasn't from pain—not in his hip anyway.

"Jesus," he said, "come up here."

She released him, looked up at him from between his legs.

"Up where?"

"Up here where I can get to you."

"Ooh," she said, "this sounds like fun."

She moved up so he could get to her with his hands— but then she said, "Wait, I have an idea."

She put a leg on either side of his head and squatted over his face. He could see the muscles on the inside of her thigh, knew she'd be able to stay like that for a long time.

She lowered her fragrant pussy to his mouth, pressed it to him. He stuck out his tongue, licked her until she was so wet his face was sopping, as well. And still he went on, using his tongue and his lips, taking her smooth buttocks in his hands, relieving some of the pressure on her thighs and calves. She rubbed herself over his face, harder and harder until she gasped, tensed, and gushed . . .

Later still she squatted over him again, only this time it was right over his rigid cock. She reached down to hold him in place, and then slid the length of him inside her. She did this with her back to him, thinking she could keep most of her weight off him this way. He also found it fascinating to watch as her ass bounced up and down on him, and his cock went in and out. He'd never before had such a clear view of the action, and he found it quite stimulating. Enough so that he lasted quite a long time . . .

"Look at you," she said later, laughing. "What?"

She touched his chin.

"Your chin is rubbed raw from my hair."

She leaned over and kissed his chin, then his mouth. He was the man she had been waiting for, for a long time. Even though he couldn't move because of his hip, he was better than any man she'd ever been with.

"Can I sleep here?" she asked. "I'm tired."

"Sure."

"And then we can go again."

"After we both get some sleep," he said.

FORTY-THREE

When there was a knock on the door, it was Cynthia who answered it. She pulled on her shirt, and he watched her long legs as she walked to the door.

"It's Detective Fellows," she said.

"Let him in—if you don't mind."

She laughed and opened the door wide so Fellows could enter.

"Thank you, Mrs. Bodeen. How're you doin', Clint?"

"Doctor says nothing's broken," Clint said. "I'll heal. How about you?"

Fellows held up his hands, which were bandaged.

"Not too bad."

"Still got a job?"

"Oh, yeah," the detective said. "The chief's happy we got the killer. He thinks that's the end of it."

"Only time will tell," Clint said. "Whoever he was working for might keep trying, send somebody else. We'll have to wait and see."

"Unless we find him," Fellows said.

"That's right, unless we find him."

"I can be out of this bed by morning," Clint told him.

"Well, I may be able to find him before that," Fellows said.

"How?"

"By proving again that I'm good at this detective stuff."

"Go ahead, prove it."

"It might put you at risk."

Clint laughed and shook his head.

"What else is new?"

Both men turned away while Cynthia got herself dressed. Clint did it only as a courtesy to Fellows, so the man wouldn't feel awkward.

"Okay, you can turn around," she told them.

When they did, she looked impeccable, unlike a woman who had spent the afternoon having sex.

"Cynthia, you're sure about Patrick?"

"My husband would like the university project to go away," she said. "He'll bluster and threaten, but he hasn't the nerve to do anything about it."

"What about the foreman?" Fellows asked.

"He'll generally do what he's told, but he doesn't have much imagination. He has no cause to sabotage a major building project."

"And you?" Fellows asked quietly.

She laughed. "I'm flattered that you ask, Detective, but as long as I have enough money to spend—and an occasional lover or two—I'm pretty happy with what I've got." She gave Clint a very pointed look.

"What about your horse?" Clint asked. "We tracked it from the construction site right into your barn."

Cynthia smiled. "What about it? I never denied that I rode out there. But I had nothing to do with setting fires—at least not the kind that damages property."

"Who was driving the buckboard?" Fellows persisted. "We found two sets of tracks—one belonging to your horse and the other made by a buckboard and horse."

"His name is my secret," she told him emphatically. "But I assure you he had nothing to do with the trouble out at the university."

There was strength in her words, but then Clint noticed a brief sadness come into her eyes. It disappeared in an instant, but suddenly he knew—it was Fitz. He and Cynthia could have met out at the building site, then parted ways on the road afterward. He'd mentioned that he had a room in town.

"I believe you," Clint said quietly. "And I believed you when you said your husband had nothing to do with the vandalism."

"Thank you." Cynthia nodded, and a moment of understanding passed between them. So not only had Clint lost his friend, but Cynthia had lost a lover. And the killer was still at large.

"Right now, though," Clint went on, "you better leave before we talk about what we have in mind."

"That will give me deniability, huh?"

"Exactly," Fellows said.

"I'll see you again, Clint," she said. "I'll continue to . . . nurse you back to health."

"Fred, why don't you walk the lady downstairs?" Clint suggested.

"Why?" Fellows asked. "I mean, not that I'm not a gentleman—"

"In case you haven't notice," Clint said, "I'm naked under this sheet. I need to put something on. And you need to make some . . . arrangements?"

"Oh, all right," Fellows said. "Mrs. Bodeen?"

"Cynthia, Detective," she said, "just call me Cynthia."

"Yes, ma'am."

FORTY-FOUR

The word certainly had gone around that Clint and Detective Fellows had caught and killed the man responsible for sabotaging the university construction and killing Ted Fitzgerald. This caused George Eiland much anxiety. He'd hired the killer and had put all his confidence in the man. Once the project was held up indefinitely, he'd find a way to make off with what remained of the money—a still significant amount that would absolve him of all his gambling debts. And up until today, that confidence had been warranted—the money he had paid the man was worth it. But nothing was worth it if the law found out that he had hired him.

The word had circulated that Clint Adams had been injured and was in bed in his room. The word also spread that the killer had talked to Adams, who would testify when he was able to get out of bed.

Eiland sat in his room until well after dark, fretting. He did not have the time to go out and find himself another killer. If Clint Adams was to be silenced, he was going to have to do it himself. Not one accustomed to gunplay, he had to work up the nerve. He had a .32 caliber pistol in his possession, because that was what men were supposed to do in the West, carry a pistol, but he had never had occasion to use it.

There didn't seem to be any other choice.

Clint lay in his bed in the dark. Fellows was in another room, waiting. Clint's gun was not hanging on the bedpost. The empty holster was, but he had his gun in his hand, and his door was unlocked. Whoever had hired the killer had no choice. He either had to get out of town, or try to kill Clint.

Fellows had grabbed another policeman to help. He was stationed in the lobby with instructions to stop anyone—anyone, man or woman—who tried to leave the building.

Clint had his trousers back on, was sitting with his back to the bedpost. Hopefully, if and when his door opened, he'd be able to react quickly enough. Taking cover would be a problem—he was even sure he could roll himself out of bed—so it would all depend on how quickly and accurately he could shoot.

As he heard the floorboards outside his room creaking, and the doorknob squeaking a little as someone tried turning it slowly, he thought about how many times his life had depended on this in the past, and he was still here.

And he certainly didn't want to die before Cynthia Bodeen finished nursing him back to health . . .

Watch for

FORTY MILE RIVER

369th novel in the exciting GUNSMITH series
from Jove

Coming in September!

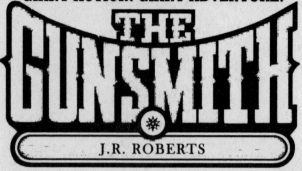

J GIANT ACTION! GIANT ADVENTURE!

THE GUNSMITH

J.R. ROBERTS

penguin.com/actionwesterns